All Around the World

Contents

Introduction

I often think that writing a short story is a bit like building a house. Each word is a brick. We write one sentence – a row of bricks. Then we write another sentence on top of it. And another one. The sentences become a wall – a paragraph. Then we move on to the next wall – more rows of sentences, until we have a house or a story.

There are big differences, of course, between building a house and writing a story. When builders start, they know exactly what the house will look like. They have it planned. They know how many bricks they will need, how high the walls should go, where the doors and windows will be.

Writers don't know how many words they will need. They might have a plan but they don't know exactly what is going to happen. They hope for the best and start, but the story – the house – might collapse before they get to the end.

Seven different builders with the same plan

will build the same house seven times. Seven writers will never write the same story. They might use many of the same words, they might write about the same subject – love, say, or the end of love – but how they use the words, how they build the walls, will always be different. There will be seven very different stories.

Where do the words – the bricks – come from? They come from all of us – people who talk, people who live, people who use words every day. The writers take the words – our words – and build unique stories, using the words that we give them.

In this book, *All Around the World*, there are seven stories, from very different places: Japan, Ireland, Ukraine, Holland, Somalia – and mid-air. Seven writers wrote them but everyone in the world, everyone who uses words – you, the reader – helped to create them.

Roddy Doyle, 2026

Until the Girl Died

by Anne Enright

The girl died.

Well, what was that to me? The girl died. And it was nothing to do with us, with either of us. She died the stupid way that people do – in a car crash, in Italy. Where, presumably, she was driving on the wrong side of the road.

Silly twit.

If the girl had not died then she would not have mattered in the slightest. She would have been a lapse; my husband is prone to lapses – less often of late, but yes, once every couple of years he does lapse, after the office party say, or travelling on business. I don't think he visits prostitutes – I mean, some men do, some men must. Or quite a lot of men must, actually – but my husband doesn't. And I know, I know, I would say that, but . . .

I've thought about this a lot over the years; things catch my eye in articles, in magazines.

I have wondered, what makes them go and what makes them stay, what do they want, men? It's the great mystery, isn't it? What men 'want'. And the damage they might do to get it.

The things you read in the papers.

'Oh, sure they're all the same.' Isn't that what your mother used to say? 'They're all the same.'

But they're not. They have their reasons and they have their limits. They have hearts, too. And I can say, without a shadow of a doubt, that my husband is not the kind of man to buy sex in the street. He likes intimacy. That is what he craves. My husband is the kind of man who will always look you in the eye. He loves women – even older ones. He loves to talk to them, and make them feel good, and he loves to kiss them, and be a little dangerous; it makes him feel so young. And he also loves me.

He is not a bastard, that is what I am saying. I am saying that he is a fantastic man. My husband is a fantastic man. And until the girl died, beetling along in her little Renault Clio on the wrong side of a road in Tuscany, until the girl died, that was enough for me. To be married to a fantastic man who loved me, and was prone, once in a long while, to a little lapse and a lot of Catholic guilt about it.

Isn't it worth it? I used to say. Isn't it bloody

worth it for the bunch of flowers and the new coat and maybe shoes? Isn't it bloody worth it for a long weekend with the kids, all of us together in Ballybunion, walking the winter beach? A couple of bottles of wine in the evening and more sex than is decent at our age, with my wonderful husband. Home again after his little lapse with some overambitious young one who will Shortly. Be. Fired. Thank you darling and, no, I know you will never do it again.

But actually I hated it. It was like living on a page of some horrible Sunday newspaper. Horrible people. Horrible people with their horrible sex lives and their horrible money.

No.

He works hard, my husband. And I have always been a great asset to him. And we are ordinary people. And I am proud of that too.

Ke . . . I can't say his name. Isn't that funny?

It is quite an ordinary name, I say it fifteen times a day. Mind you, he never calls me anything back. Isn't that the way of it? What do men call their wives. 'Em . . .' Like every woman on the planet was christened Emily.

'Em . . . is that shirt clean?'

The girl was called – listen to this – Samantha.

Not that I knew this at the time. Not that I knew anything at the time.

And she was only referred to by name because she died. If it hadn't been for the car crash she would have been, and always remained, that young one in IT, or even that slapper over in IT.

I'm sorry.

But.

The poor child, who thought it was a laugh to sleep with my husband – and it is a laugh, God knows I have laughed enough myself – the poor child, who thought it was a laugh to sleep with the father of my three children, did something worse than all that. She went and died on him too. She went and died on us all.

Of course, I didn't have a clue.

He came home – when I think about it, it must have been the day he'd heard the news – and he sat on the sofa, and for the first time since his mother's funeral, I saw him cry. The children saw him cry. I had no idea what he was crying for. I felt like calling an ambulance. Then I put two and two together and realised he must be lapsing again, he must be mid-lapse. And I panicked.

I know that. I did panic. And It's not like me. He lifted his head to speak to me and I said,

'I don't want to know.' That was all. 'I don't want to know.'

And I said it really fast. Like what was

happening was not actually happening. Or he'd better make bloody sure it wasn't happening because I wasn't having the mess of it all over my beautiful, hard-won house. And he pushed his face around to clear away the tears – not hot tears, not outraged, grief-stricken tears, just that leaky, worn-out water you find on your face sometimes, when you are sick or defeated – he wiped the tears away and then he just sat.

My fantastic man.

The first time he lapsed, at a guess, was when the children were small. I was up to my tonsils in nappies and mayhem, falling asleep before my head hit the pillow, fat as a fool. Anyway. They feel 'excluded', fathers; isn't that what the articles say? They have the weight of the world on their shoulders, and after a while – I'm convinced of this – they start to resent you, maybe even to hate you. Then, one day, they love you madly again and you realise – slowly, you realise – that they have been up to something. They've had a fright. They've come running back home.

Which is nice, too. In a way.

Oh, what the hell.

The first time it happened, my father was in hospital having some tests, actually, and I was far too busy to shout at my husband, or go through his pockets, or sniff at his clothes before

I put them in the washing machine. I had more important things on my mind.

In the end, everything went so well, Daddy didn't even have to have chemo – after which, I was too relieved to double back and start shouting at my husband, or sniffing at his clothes. It was over by then, and besides, I had learned something about myself. I'd learned that I was not the type to rage and scream. And that was an odd kind of feeling, I must say. Because I grew up with the same dreams as every other girl, but when the chips were down . . . When the chips were down, I kept my head held high.

What was I supposed to do?

One part of me thought he deserved a holiday, to be honest; that if I had the chance I might take one myself. Another part of me thought, 'Someone must die'. I really thought I might kill someone for this. I might kill her. Or I might kill him. Or I might leave them to it and kill myself. Well, that's no use, is it? This stupidity of my husband's was too small to bother about. But it was too large to leave us all still alive.

So maybe it was in my head, from that time. In both our heads. The idea that someone must die.

So what are we looking at? Two or three more girls, over the course of the years? A scattering of 'accidents', and then, one day, this, whatever it is. A man crying on the sofa. Grief.

It was half past five. The children were watching telly before tea. I cleared them out of there – my daughter, the apple of her father's eye, welling up a bit herself at the tragic look of him, with his coat thrown beside him and his briefcase still in the other hand.

Kids bury that sort of stuff very deep. I thought it would be better if she talked about it, but when I asked her, a week later, about her father crying on the sofa she just looked at me, like I had landed in from outer space.

'What sofa?' she said. 'Which sofa?'

That's Shauna for you, who is nine. There's no point talking to her brothers about it, they've already gone into the grunting phase.

And then I think, Why not? Why not talk to your sons about things? Why not rear men who can speak?

Because there was my husband on the sofa, staring mortality in the face. And what else? His own smallness. Looking as though he had killed her himself, although he had not killed her, he had not even loved her. Thinking (as I imagine) about some beautiful part of her, mangled by the door or bonnet, and turning already to clay.

And there is no one he can talk to about this. No one at all.

Men don't have friends like that – guys you might ring and say, 'Take him out for a drink. Talk it over. Sort him out.' No. The only friend he has is me.

And he can't tell me, because I really do not want to know.

All this in hindsight, of course. At the time, I looked at him and I thought that our marriage was finished, or that he was finished. I was looking at him on extended sick leave and then what? My husband crying on the sofa was forty-nine years old. And if you think forty-nine is a tough station, try fifty-five.

I was looking at a long future with a man who had forgotten what he was for.

So when he pushes the tears off his face with his hand, and when he lifts his face to tell me all about it, there is only one thing I can say to him, and that is:

'I don't want to know.'

How did we get through the next week? Normally, at a guess. That's how we did it. We got through the week in a completely normal way. While I waited for some hint or clue. The back page of the paper that he stares at too hard and too long. And then, on Tuesday morning, I come in from the school run and he's still there, in his dark suit, putting on his funeral tie.

'Who's dead?'

'Some girl,' he says.

'What girl? Someone's daughter?' He doesn't answer. He brushes his shoulders off in the mirror.

He says, 'We get them trained up, and the next thing, they're gone.'

'Well, I'm sure she didn't mean to.'

Round and round goes the funeral tie, down through the knot. Pull it tight, ease it a little loose again. Kiss the wife goodbye.

'You don't want me to come?' I say, because I am raging now. I know what has happened, now. I want to twist the knife.

'No,' he says. 'She's only with us a year.'

'You sure?'

'No, no.' I watch you pick up your briefcase, pull your phone off the charger, check for your keys.

'Home for tea?' I say.

'What is it?'

'I thought I'd grill a bit of salmon.'

I see you forget where your good coat is kept, open one door of the wardrobe, the other door of the wardrobe, look to your wife who says, 'It's under the stairs.'

Look your wife in the eye as she says this, reach out to touch her neck and hair.

Say, 'Thanks,' then off you go.

Oh, I know what you are thanking me for.

The front door clicks shut on my husband in his funeral tie and I wander downstairs to tidy away the breakfast things and make my usual cup of coffee. I fill the kettle and plug it in. I take out my mug and put it on the counter. And then, before the water is boiled, I have the recycling bin spilt all over the floor, and I'm going through the old newspapers for death notices.

Samantha 'Sammy' MacHale, tragically, abroad.

Easy. I get out the phone book and look that up too.

The church is in Walkinstown, so that's her family off the Cromwellsfort Road. She might have lived at home still, at twenty-four – the price of everything these days. I could go there now, if I wanted to. I could drive there in my little car. I wonder do her parents know what she got up to? I have a shameful desire to tell them – so sharp, I have to stand still until it subsides.

I am not that kind of person.

No.

I make my cup of coffee and I calm down.

Still, I wonder what she looked like. What

school did she go to; do they have pictures in the corridors, of former girls in a row, the class of – what year would she be? – the class of 1998.

So young.

Who could be that young?

All the time I am loading the dishwasher and pulling out the hoover and doing my morning chores, the funeral is happening in my head. But I am not going to jump in the car and hack my way across town to Walkinstown. I am not that kind of person. I am not going to panic at the last minute and show up at the cemetery to check the faces at the grave and pick up a few words here and there, about what a fine girl she was, 'irrepressible', 'full of fun'. Bloody right she was full of fun.

Or not. Maybe she was shy, unassuming. Easily impressed. She might have been a quiet kind of girl. A girl who was anxious to please.

No.

I am not going to find this out, or anything else. Because that would be obscene. I am not going to show up like a ghost at the wedding – what's the opposite of that? – like a flesh and blood wife, at this last dance with the dead.

We had the salmon when he came home. Potatoes. A bit of asparagus.

'Lovely,' says my husband. 'Delicious.' Then

he gets up afterwards and makes himself a sausage sandwich, cold from the fridge. Butter, mayonnaise, the lot.

And I say, 'Why don't you stick some lard in there, while you're at it?'

This is the last real thing I say to him, for a long while. *Where's the gas bill gone when will you be home would you pick up Shauna from her ballet?* We could do this for ever. After a few weeks of it, my husband gets a nervous cough: he wonders if it could be lung cancer. His toe is numb, isn't that a sign of MS? And I just say, 'Get it checked out.' Because the girl is dead. So let's not bother with the fuss and fuckology of getting back together. Let's not do all that again. Not this time. This time let us mourn.

I am too proud. I know that. And in my pride I watched him – my fantastic, stupid man – lurch around in his life. And I did not offer him a helping hand.

Where's the key to the shed when will you be home would you buy a pack of plastic blades for the Flymo?

The girl was with us, all this time. Dead or alive. She was standing at the bus stop on the corner, she was sitting in our living room watching Big Brother, she was being buried, night after night, on the evening news.

I think that milk's gone off when will you be home I really don't want the children having TV sets in their rooms.

After a month of this, I looked at my husband and saw that he was old. It did not happen overnight; it happened over thirty nights or so. My husband shaking hands with death. And what else? Thinking about it. Thinking it wouldn't be so bad to be dead, after all. Like she was.

Whenever I woke in the night, he was awake too. Once I heard him crying again; this time in the shower. He thought the noise of the water would cover it. I listened to him snuffling and choking in the spray and I realised it was time to put my pride away. It was time to call him back home.

On Saturday, after the supermarket run, I put on my good coat and my leather gloves. And a hat, even – my funeral hat. And when my husband said, 'Where are you off to?' – because God knows I never go anywhere without drawing a map – I said, 'I'm going to visit a grave.'

I had a beautiful bunch of white lilies, all wrapped up in cellophane. I picked them off the kitchen counter and walked past him – I cradled the lilies against my shoulder and I walked past my husband, who was now old – and I did not look back, as I went out the door.

She did not matter to him, I know that. I know she did not matter. So I went to the cemetery and sought out her grave. I wandered through the headstones until I found her, and I put the lilies on the ground under which she lay, and I told her that she mattered. Then I went home and said to my husband:

'Let's do something for Easter, what do you think? Something nice. Where would you like to go?'

Afternoon at the Bakery

by Yoko Ogawa
translated by Stephen Snyder

It was a beautiful Sunday. The sky was a cloudless dome of sunlight. Out on the square, leaves fluttered in a gentle breeze along the pavement. Everything seemed to glimmer: the roof of the ice-cream stand, the tap on the drinking fountain, the eyes of a stray cat, even the base of the clock tower covered with pigeon droppings.

Families and tourists strolled through the square, enjoying the weekend. Squeaky sounds could be heard from a man who was twisting balloon animals. A circle of children watched him, entranced.

Nearby, a woman sat on a bench knitting. Somewhere a horn sounded. A flock of pigeons burst into the air and startled a baby who began to cry. The mother hurried over to gather the child in her arms. You could gaze at this perfect picture all day – an afternoon bathed in light and comfort – and perhaps never notice a single detail out of place.

As I pushed through the revolving door of the bakery and walked inside, the noise of the square was instantly muffled, and replaced by the sweet scent of vanilla. The shop was empty.

'Excuse me,' I called hesitantly. There was no reply, so I decided to sit down on a stool in the corner and wait.

It was my first time in the bakery, a neat, clean, modest little shop. Cakes, pies and chocolates were carefully arranged in a glass case, and tins of biscuits lined shelves on either side. On the counter behind the register was a roll of pretty orange and light blue chequered wrapping paper. Everything looked delicious. But I knew before I entered the shop what I would buy: two strawberry shortcakes. That was all.

The bell in the clock tower rang four times. Once more a flock of pigeons rose into the sky and flew across the square, settling in front of the flower shop. The florist came out with a scowl on her face and a mop to drive them away, and a flurry of grey feathers wafted into the air.

There was no sign of anyone in the shop, and after waiting a little while longer I considered giving up and leaving. But I had only recently moved to this town and I did not know of another good bakery. Perhaps the fact that they could keep customers waiting like this was a sign of confidence, rather than rudeness. The light in the glass display case was pleasant and soft, the pastries looked beautiful and the stool was quite comfortable – I liked the place, in spite of the service.

A short, plump woman stepped through the revolving door. Noise from the square filtered in behind her and faded away. 'Is anybody here?' she called out. 'Where could she have gone?' she added, turning and smiling at me. 'She must be out on an errand. I'm sure she'll be right back.'

She sat down next to me and I gave a little bow. 'I suppose I could get behind the counter and serve you myself,' the woman said. 'I know pretty well how things work around here. I sell them their spices.'

'That's very kind of you, but I'm not in a hurry,' I said.

We waited together. She rearranged her scarf, tapped the toe of her shoe and anxiously fidgeted with the clasp on a black leather bag – apparently used to collect her accounts. I realised she was trying to come up with a topic for conversation.

'The cakes here are delicious,' she said at last. 'They use our spices, so you know there's nothing funny in them.'

'That's reassuring,' I said.

'The place is usually very busy. Strange that it's so empty today. There's often a line outside.'

People passed by the shop window – young couples, old men, tourists, a policeman on patrol – but no one seemed interested in the bakery. The woman turned to look out at the square, and ran her fingers through her wavy white hair. Whenever she moved in her seat, she gave off an odd smell; the scent of medicinal herbs and overripe fruit mingled with the vinyl of her apron. It reminded me of when I was a child, and the smell of the little greenhouse in the garden where my father used to grow orchids. I was strictly forbidden to open the door; but once, without permission, I did. The scent of the orchids was not at all disagreeable, and this pleasant link to my past made me like the old woman.

'I was happy to see they have strawberry shortcake,' I said, pointing at the case. 'They're the real thing. None of that jelly, or too much fruit piled on top, or those little figurines they use for decoration. Just strawberries and cream.'

'You're right,' she said. 'I can guarantee they're good. The best thing in the shop. The base is made with our special vanilla.'

'I'm buying them for my son. Today is his birthday.'

'Really? Well, I hope it's a happy one. How old is he?'

'Six. He'll always be six. He's dead.' I explained.

He died twelve years ago. Suffocated in an abandoned fridge left in an empty bit of land. When I first saw him, I didn't think he was dead. I thought he was just ashamed to look me in the eye because he had stayed away from home for three days. An old woman I had never seen before was standing nearby, looking dazed, and I realised that she must have been the one who had found him. Her hair was all messed up, her face pale, and her lips were trembling. She looked more dead than my son.

'I'm not angry, you know,' I said to him. 'Come here and let me give you a hug. I bought the shortcake for your birthday. Let's go back to the house.'

But he didn't move. He had curled up to fit between the shelves and the egg box, with his legs carefully folded and his face tucked between his knees. The curve of his spine disappeared into a dark, cramped space behind him. The skin on his neck caught the light from the open door. It was so smooth, covered in soft down – I knew it all too well.

'No, it couldn't be,' I said to the old woman. 'He's just sleeping. He hasn't eaten anything, and he must be exhausted. Let's carry him home and try not to wake him. He should sleep, as much as he wants. He'll wake up later, I'm sure of it.' But the woman did not answer.

The reaction of the woman in the shop to my story was unlike anything I'd encountered in the past. There was no sign of sympathy or surprise or even embarrassment on her face. I would have known if she was merely pretending to respond so calmly. The experience of losing my son had taught me to read people, and I could tell immediately that this woman was genuine. She neither regretted having asked me the question nor blamed me for confessing something so personal to a stranger.

'Well,' she said, 'then it was lucky you chose this bakery. There are no better pastries anywhere; your son will be pleased. And they include a whole box of birthday candles for free. They're lovely – red, blue, pink, yellow, some with flowers or butterflies, animals, anything you could want.'

She smiled faintly, in a way that seemed perfectly suited to the quiet of the bakery. I found myself wondering whether she actually understood that my son had died. Or perhaps she knew only too well about people dying.

Long after I had realised that my son would not be coming back, I kept the strawberry shortcake we were meant to have eaten together. I passed my days watching it rot. First, the cream turned brown and separated from the fat, staining the cellophane wrapper. Then the strawberries dried out, wrinkling up like the heads of deformed babies. The sponge cake hardened and crumbled, and finally a layer of mould appeared.

'Mould can be quite beautiful,' I told my husband. The spots multiplied, covering the shortcake in delicate blotches of colour.

'Get rid of it,' my husband said.

I could tell he was angry. But I could not understand why he spoke so harshly about our son's birthday cake. So I threw it in his face. Mould and crumbs covered his hair and his cheeks, and a terrible smell filled the room. It was like breathing in death.

Here, in the bakery, the strawberry shortcakes were displayed right on the upper shelf of the pastry case, the most prominent place in the shop. Each was topped with three whole strawberries. They looked perfectly preserved, no sign of mould.

'I think I'll be going,' the old woman said. She stood up, smoothed her apron, and glanced out the window toward the square, as though looking one last time for the return of the bakery shop girl.

'I'll wait a little longer,' I said.

'You do that,' she said, reaching out to gently touch my hand. Hers was hardened and wrinkled – made rough by her work – and she had dirt under her fingernails. Still, her hand was warm and comforting, perhaps like the heat from those little birthday candles she had mentioned.

'I'm going to check on a couple of places where the girl might be, and if I find her I'll tell her to come straight back.'

'Thank you,' I said.

'Not at all . . . Goodbye.'

Clutching her bag under her arm, she turned to leave. As she stepped through the revolving door, I noticed that her apron strings were coming untied in the back. I tried to stop her, but I was too late. She disappeared into the crowd in the square, and I was alone again.

My son had been an intelligent child. He could read his favourite picture book from beginning to end aloud without making a single mistake. He would use a different voice for each character – the piglet, the prince, the robot, the old man. He was left-handed. He had a broad forehead and a mole on one earlobe. When I was busy making dinner, he would often ask questions I did not know how to answer. 'Who invented Chinese characters?' 'Why do people grow?' 'What is air?' 'Where do we go when we die?'

After he was gone, I began to go to the library and gather articles from every newspaper and magazine about children who had died tragically, and make copies of them.

An eleven-year-old girl who was raped and buried in a forest.

A nine-year-old boy who had been kidnapped and later found in a wine crate with both of his ankles cut off.

A ten-year-old who had been on a tour of an ironworks but slipped from a catwalk and was instantly dissolved in the furnace.

I would read these articles aloud, reciting them like poems.

Suddenly I noticed something in the bakery. How had I not seen this before? I rose slightly from my seat and looked past the counter. A doorway behind the till was half open, and I could see into the kitchen. A young woman was standing inside with her face turned away. I was about to call out to her, but I stopped myself. She was talking to someone on the telephone, and she was crying.

I couldn't hear anything, but I could see her shoulders trembling. Her hair had been gathered carelessly under a white cap. Despite some spots of cream and chocolate, her apron looked neat and pressed. Her slight frame seemed almost that of a little girl.

The kitchen was as neatly arranged as the shop. Bowls, knives, mixers, pastry bags, sifters – everything needed was right where it should be. The dishcloths were clean and dry, the floor spotless. And in the middle of it stood the girl, her sadness perfectly at home in the tidy kitchen. I could hear nothing, not a word, not a sound. Her hair swayed slightly with her sobs. She was looking down at the counter, her body leaning against the oven. Her right hand clutched a napkin. I couldn't see the expression on her face, but her misery was clear from the clench of her jaw, her pale neck, and the tense grip of her fingers on the telephone.

The reason she was crying didn't matter to me. Perhaps there was no reason. Her tears had that sort of purity.

One day it occurred to me that I needed to experience the same suffering he had. The door that would not open no matter how hard you pushed, no matter how long you pounded on it. The screams no one heard. Darkness, hunger, pain. Slow suffocation.

First, I turned off our refrigerator and emptied it: last night's potato salad, ham, eggs, cabbage, cucumbers, wilted spinach, yoghurt, some cans of beer, pork – I pulled everything out and threw it aside. The ketchup spilled, eggs broke, ice cream melted. But the refrigerator was empty now, so I took a deep breath, curled myself into a ball, and slowly worked my way inside.

As the door closed, all light vanished. I could no longer tell whether my eyes were open or shut, and I realised that it made no difference in here. The walls of the refrigerator were still cool. Where does death come from, I asked myself?

'What do you think you're doing?' my husband said as he ripped open the refrigerator door.

'I'm going to him.' I tried to brush away his shaking hand and close the door again.

'That's enough,' he said, pulling me from the refrigerator. He slapped my face. Then he left me.

Not one person in the crowd on the square knew that a young woman was crying in the kitchen behind the bakery. I was the only witness. The afternoon sunlight streaming in through the window had darkened, as the sun began to dip below the roof of the town hall. The man on the square with the popular balloon animals performed now for only a few children. A group of people had gathered around the clock tower to take pictures of the mechanical show as the bell struck five.

I knew I had only to call out to the girl, and then I could make my purchase and leave, but I stopped myself. Her starched apron was slightly too large, which made her seem all the more small and vulnerable. I noticed the sweat on her neck, her wrinkled cuffs and long fingers, and I imagined how she must look when she is working. I could see her taking the steaming sponge cakes from the oven, piping on the cream, and arranging each strawberry with total care. I was certain she would make the finest shortcakes in the world.

Several years after my son died, when I began living alone, I received an odd phone call. The voice was unfamiliar but clearly that of a young man. He sounded a little nervous, yet he spoke politely as he mentioned my son's name.

'What?' I gasped, for a moment paralysed.

'Is he at home?' he said.

'No, he's not,' I managed to say.

'Well then . . . I just wanted to speak to him about the reunion. For our middle school class. Do you know when he'll be back?'

I told him he wasn't home, that he was studying abroad.

'Oh, that's too bad,' he said. 'I was looking forward to seeing him.' He sounded genuinely disappointed.

'Were you friends?'

'Yes. We were in the drama club together. He was president and I was vice president.'

'The drama club?'

'We won the city competition and went on to the national finals. You remember, we did *Man of Flame*. He played Van Gogh, and I played his brother, Theo. He was always the leading man, the ladies' man, and I was his sidekick. Not just on stage but in life. He was always in the limelight.'

Somehow it didn't bother me that he was talking about a completely different person. Nor did I try to correct him. My son had read his picture books so well that it seemed quite likely he might have had a leading role in a play one day.

'Is he still acting?'

'Yes—'

'Really? I thought so. Could you tell him I called?'

'Of course, I will.'

After he had hung up, I held the phone to my ear for a moment, listening to the hum of the dial tone. I never heard from him again.

The bell in the clock tower began to ring. A flock of pigeons lifted into the sky. As the fifth chime sounded, a door beneath the clock opened and a little parade of animated models appeared – a few soldiers, a chicken and a skeleton. Since the clock was very old, the models were slightly discoloured, their movements stiff and awkward. The chicken's head swivelled about as if to squawk; the skeleton danced. And then, from the door, an angel appeared, beating her golden wings.

The girl in the kitchen put the phone down. I held my breath. She looked down at the phone for a moment, then she heaved a deep sigh and dabbed at her tears with the napkin. I repeated to myself what I would say when she emerged into the fading light of the shop:

'Two strawberry shortcakes, please.'

The Buggy

by Roddy Doyle

There were people at the far end of the beach. Some adults, a lot of children. An extended family, maybe – he didn't know. He tried to see if one of the adults was carrying a baby or if there was a toddler – a padded lump – plonked on the sand.

He didn't want to walk over, down from the path, across the sand and stones, to the buggy. It was facing the sea. If the people up the beach had been nearer to it, he'd have known that it was theirs. He'd have known that they'd parked the buggy there at the edge of the sea so the baby would drink in the air – the ozone, whatever it was – and sleep, and stay asleep for a while. But it stood out, alone. There wasn't an adult or a sibling, a towel or a bucket, anywhere near it. It made no sense.

It was more than likely empty. That didn't make much sense, either, a buggy abandoned on the beach like that. But he remembered abandoning a buggy himself, years ago – it would have been more than thirty years – when the frame had buckled as he was pushing it up the hill in that place in France they'd gone to on their way to the ferry. Mont-Saint-Michel. A tiny island with steep streets leading to some kind of church at the top.

It had been a spectacular place, dripping with history and religion, but all he remembered about it was the ache in his arms, and the heat, as he pushed the buggy and the toddler in it up the hill. He remembered the metallic screech as the frame – the sides – surrendered and the toddler seemed to disappear, as if she had been eaten by the buggy. The toddler, Gráinne, was fine – she had a toddler of her own these days – but the buggy wasn't saveable. No amount of bending or hammering would have coaxed it back into shape. They'd left it beside a bin and passed three more buggies, buckled and discarded, on their way back down to the car park.

Maybe that was what had happened here. The frame had given up as the buggy was pushed – shoved, forced – across the sand. But he was looking at it and he knew: there was nothing wrong with this one. It was a solid-looking thing; a small adult could have squeezed into it. A hen or a stag party – he could picture the other eejits pushing a little bride or groom from one pub to the next in the buggy he was looking at.

Was the tide coming in or on its way out? He didn't know. He hadn't paid much attention to the tides and their times since he was a kid. He remembered how much he'd loved looking them up in the back of his father's *Independent*, after his father had shown him how to read the charts.

The sea – the wave he was looking at now – stopped a yard, a metre, from the buggy's front wheels, and receded. He waited for the next wave. Exactly the same – from where he stood. It got no closer to the wheels. He looked again, from left to right, to see if anyone was going to claim the buggy before the sea took it.

He should have kept driving. Of course, he should have. He'd been on his way to meet his brother, who'd moved down to Arklow. He'd left the house early – hours early – before he'd wanted to. He'd just been anxious – anxious about finding his brother's place, anxious about the traffic, anxious about leaving the house, anxious about meeting his brother. He'd seen the sign for the beach and he'd turned left, off the motorway. And here he was, about to witness a drowning, an abandonment. Something bad. Something dreadful. An accusation, a misunderstanding, a night in a police station, a slot on the news. Or just an empty buggy on a cold Irish beach. A mystery. A story he didn't want to make up, or even think about.

He should have kept driving. He shouldn't have left home in the first place.

He didn't want to do it – he really didn't. He'd go over now to the buggy; he'd look in, he'd bend down. Even here, on the path above the beach, he could feel it. The magic, the curse – the man he'd been thirty years ago. The man who would have known what to do. The man who wouldn't have hesitated. But he was so far away from being that man, he'd have to turn into an entirely different man – a man who wasn't in him.

He could remember being a kid. He remembered being very small. He could remember looking up at the handle of the fridge, in the kitchen. He could remember standing beside his father, resting his arm on his father's knee as his father ate his dinner. He could remember the smell of his father's tobacco. He could remember the paint on his father's trousers. He could remember his father telling his mother that he'd change his trousers after he'd finished his dinner; his father said he was starving and the grub wouldn't taste any better in clean trousers, the trousers weren't the ones eating it. He remembered his mother laughing and calling his father an eejit. He remembered looking up at them – their words and laughter – over his head.

That was how far back he could go. But not just that – the little lad was still in him. He was the much, much older version of that child. And the older boys, the other layers of his life – they were in him, too. Not just the memories – it wasn't that they were vivid. They were living things, events – he could live them now. He could scratch at the blue paint on his father's cord trousers. He could hear his mother's laughter – now he could. He could feel his foot hitting a wet leather football. He could hear the chalk on a primary-school blackboard. He could taste the first girl's tongue – he could feel her sweat on his cheek as they kissed, both of them afraid to stop, like they were both cycling bikes for the first time and would fall off if they slowed down or stopped.

But the man – the competent young man he'd been, the father – he couldn't feel him at all.

He could see him. He could see that younger version of himself take Gráinne from the buggy that time as he pushed her up the hill at Mont

St Michel, making a joke of its collapse, making her brothers laugh – *The poor ol' buggy; your bum was too big for it, Gráinne* – and carrying her back down the hill. But he couldn't feel her weight on his arm, or the confidence – the knowledge – that he'd make it all the way without changing arms or putting her down and trying to persuade her to walk.

He could remember another buggy. He was standing on the platform as a train came slowly into Killester station, with his sons on either side of him. A double buggy this time – before Gráinne was born. He had one boy's hand in his own left hand – the younger lad, Colm – and he held the buggy, folded, in his right hand. The older boy, Seán, held on to the buggy. The train stopped. There was no one getting off, no one there to press the button to open the train door. He forgot that Seán loved pressing the button, that it was his job, the thing that made him more important than his little brother. He let go of Colm's hand for a second, to give the button a jab – and Colm was gone. Colm had tried to step onto the train; his stride fell short of the gap, and he dropped between the train and the platform, under the train. Someone had seen what had happened and was shouting up the platform to the driver, as he got down on his knees, gently grabbed Colm's outstretched hand – *Good lad, up you come* – and pulled him up to the platform, gave him a hug, Colm smiling, not a bother on him, then got himself, the boys, and the buggy onto the train, and dealt with Seán's tears.

If the train had been moving, if Colm had slid further beneath it, if the guy on the platform hadn't been there to shout the warning to the driver – all of these possibilities rattled away inside him as the train left the station and the boys sat so they could both look out the window and get ready to be surprised by any trains dashing past in the other direction.

But, really, he'd been fine, even happy. He remembered examining the soaked knees of his jeans and brushing the grit off them with his open hand. Mission accomplished.

He looked at the hand now, his right hand. It wasn't the same one – it wasn't the hand that had saved Colm. It wasn't the age, or the liver spots. It wasn't even the hand. The hand, his arm, shook sometimes – just slightly – when he had to reach out to grab something, and sometimes he was happier holding a mug or a glass in both hands till he became used to the weight.

But it wasn't his hands or his arms or ageing or anything. It was him. Just him. That phrase

from the pandemic, 'essential worker' – he'd
been an essential father. He could remember
rescuing Colm, but he couldn't imagine it – he
couldn't feel it. He couldn't believe he'd done
it. He *didn't* believe he'd done it. Or any of the
other things he'd done when he was a father.
Not just observed or witnessed, stored away for
later. Done. Picked up, set down, pushed, pulled,
fed, tickled, comforted. His physical life beyond
children, too. Ran, gasped, laughed, cried, came.
The verbs – the action words. He had the words,
but the actions? He could walk and drive and
eat and sleep. He could go through the motions.
He could get through the day.

But he didn't live.

The tide was coming in – the sea was closer
to the buggy. Another minute and the waves
would be digging under a front wheel.

There was another buggy story. He'd pushed
the buggy, empty – he couldn't remember which
buggy; they'd gone through five or six – down to
the shops, with Seán walking beside him. Seán
was grand walking anywhere, it didn't really
matter how far. But, coming back, he often went
on strike. Setting out, he'd object to the buggy –
Buggy's for babies! – but on the way home he'd
sit on the ground, plonk himself down, in pud-
dles, or right in front of shopping trolleys and pit

bulls and pensioners, and refuse to walk. Even then he objected to the buggy. He wouldn't climb into it or let his father pick him up and fasten him in.

This particular time, Seán – the adorable little bastard – shoved the buggy out onto the road, right in front of an oncoming car. The driver braked, but the car hit the buggy side-on – he'd never forget the noise, the thump. The buggy went into the air and landed clean, all four wheels at once, facing the car, and the driver, a woman with a carful of her own babies, stared out at the empty buggy and screamed and screamed and jumped out of the car and looked under it and on the roof for the missing baby – *Oh, Jesus, oh, Jesus, oh, Jesus, oh, Jesus* – while the missing baby, Seán, pointed at her and laughed. *Funneee!*

He could remember it like a scene from a film. It was a very good film. But he wasn't in it.

What happened?

Where had his life gone? Not the years – the blood. Where was the life?

The buggy on the beach was leaning over – it was going to topple. The next wave or the one after, it was going to be on its side and the baby – if there was one – would be strapped in and helpless.

If there was one.

He'd forgotten how hard moving across soft sand was; his ankles were already aching. He nearly fell – the sole of his shoe slid on a stone. He watched a wave wallop the wheel – he saw the buggy pushed back. He didn't seem to be getting any closer – he'd left it too late. His shoes were full of sand – there was a stone digging into his heel. But now the ground was more solid; there was a layer of stones, a thick band that stretched along the beach. He got over the stones quickly enough, and he was nearly at the buggy – he could feel the handle, *all* the handles, in his grip – when a wave slid up over his shoes and he was lifting his feet, moving like a mad thing, his feet smacking the water, and he caught the buggy, he grabbed one of the handles and pulled it back with him, up to the bank of stones.

He knew before he looked. He had the buggy by both handles now, and he parked it, still facing the sea. No baby. He was relieved – and disappointed – and angry. His feet were freezing – his legs, up to his knees and past them – fuckin' freezing. And he laughed. He was angry, and delighted to be angry. He was soaking and didn't know what he'd do, and he didn't care.

—Oh, God. Thank you!

It was a woman, a young woman running at him, sliding over the stones.

He checked again – the buggy was empty. He wondered why she was thanking him.

—I forgot all about it, she said.

She looked the part, the young mother, exhausted and lovely. But she didn't have a baby, on her hip or in her arms.

He held on to the buggy.

—You're drenched, she said. I'm so sorry.

He shrugged. He wasn't sure if it was a proper shrug. He was gripping the handles and leaning over the buggy, protecting the baby that wasn't in it.

She was a bit uncertain – he could see that. She'd expected him to roll the buggy across the stones to her, or to turn it around and offer her the handles. It probably looked like he needed the buggy to hold himself up. He looked down. He was wet past his trousers, halfway up his jumper.

—I left my phone in the car, she said. Are you all right?

Jesus Christ, he thought, she wanted to phone for an ambulance – for him.

He stood up straight. He let go of the buggy.

—I'm grand, he said.

—You must be frozen, she said.

His job now was to get her to stop talking to him like he was an old man. An old man who'd fallen into the water, or who'd wet himself.

—I'm grand, he said again.

He patted a buggy handle.

—Where's the owner of the vehicle? he asked.

She smiled.

—He's in the car, she said. In the car park.

—If he hasn't driven away, he said. I'm only joking.

She looked behind her, toward the car park that they couldn't see from where they stood.

—I wouldn't put it past him, she said.

He moved first. He walked off the sand, pulling the buggy with him.

—He wanted to go to the toilet like a big boy, she told him. In the dunes.

—Fair enough, he said. What's his name? I feel like I should know.

He pulled at a wet trouser leg where it was stuck to his thigh.

—Seán, she said.

—I've a Seán as well, he told her.

—Really? she said. That's amazing.

They were on the tarmac, off the sand. He let go of the buggy. She took hold of it and pointed it at the car park.

—Tell Seán I said hello, he said.

She laughed. She smiled.

—I will, she said. Bye. Thanks again.

—Seeyeh.

She hadn't asked him if he was O.K. or if he knew where he was going, or if there was someone he could phone to come and collect him. She'd seen a man who was fine, and she'd walked away. He was freezing, and stiff. He'd drive to Arklow now and change into one of his brother's tracksuits.

He took his phone from his trousers pocket and rubbed the screen dry on the shoulder of his jumper. He went to Favourites and tapped 'Seán'.

—Dad?

—Howyeh, son. Are you busy – can you talk?

—What's up? Are you all right?

He told his son about how he'd been on his way to Arklow, about how he'd been early so he'd stopped at the beach. About how he'd gone for a walk. How he'd seen the buggy facing the sea. How he'd seen the tide coming in, how he'd dashed down to the sea to rescue the buggy.

He didn't hesitate.

—There was a baby in it, Seán.

—Ah, Jesus – a baby? Are you serious?

—I couldn't believe it, he said. Fast asleep.

—No!

—Yeah.

There – in the car park beside the Irish Sea – he'd never felt happier. He watched the mother drive slowly to the gate, stop, then turn left, out, onto the road. He waved at the back of the car. A Volvo, he thought it was. Black, or very dark blue.

—Was the baby O.K.?

—Ah, yeah, he said. Not a bother on him. And come here – guess what his name was.

Flight

by David Szalay

She was very apologetic but she told the interviewer – a young woman who had flown all the way from Brazil – that she had to leave immediately.

'My daughter has just gone into labour,' she explained. 'In Seattle. The only flight they have today leaves in—' She looked at her watch. 'Exactly two hours. So I have to dash. I'm so sorry.'

'Oh,' the interviewer said. 'Well . . .'

'I'm so sorry,' Marion said again, when the woman showed no sign of moving from her sofa.

'Well would it be okay,' the interviewer asked, finally standing, 'if I emailed you some questions?'

'Of course it would. Yes, of course. I'm just going to throw some things in a suitcase,' Marion said, and she left the room.

*

She had been in the middle of answering a question when the phone had interrupted her. Something had told her not to ignore it.

The only direct flight from Toronto to Seattle that day was on one of the no-frills airlines which Marion still thought of as a new thing, though they had been around for decades.

From her narrow seat, she looked down at what was probably North Dakota. The plane swayed lightly from side to side as she peered at the pale landscape passing slowly underneath. It was hard to tell at times whether the expanse of whiteness she saw was cloud or the surface of the Earth, where people actually lived. Sometimes the dark threads of roads gave it away.

Marion was able to imagine what it would be like down there. She herself had started life in a place like that. Hard and flat, and hostile to things unless they had an obvious use. There *had* been a library in the small Manitoban town where she grew up. She had spent most of her time there when she was in her early teens. People had said of her then that she had her head in the clouds, and it was true that she had liked looking at the sky – that she had often thought it was the only thing worth looking at there.

The plane shook and tumbled over the mountains and fell through the clouds towards Seattle airport. After they had landed, Marion phoned Doug at the hospital, while waiting at the luggage carousel. He didn't answer, but phoned her back a few minutes later to tell her the news. As he told her she was jostled by someone moving forward for their luggage. She didn't notice, even when they swore at her.

She said, 'Oh Doug. How are they?'

'Okay,' he said. She thought he might have sounded happier – no doubt he was in shock, like most first-time fathers. She told him she would see him soon.

It was still only mid-afternoon, but the weather, the pouring rain, meant the light outside gave the impression of dusk.

When she arrived, Doug wasn't around. He had gone home for a while, the nurse thought, when Marion presented herself, still with her suitcase, at the maternity department somewhere high up in the hospital.

She waited – not taking a seat as she had been invited to – while the nurse went to see whether her daughter Annie was awake.

The nurse returned and told her that she was. 'Put these on please,' the nurse said, offering her what seemed to be a shoebox full of blue shower caps. It took Marion a moment to understand what they were. She sat down to stretch two of them over her shoes. When she had done that, the nurse directed her to a dispenser of disinfectant gel for her hands.

Then she said, 'Go *down* the hall, second room on your left.'

'Thank you,' Marion said, and went. With her heart thumping, she went.

She saw them through the glass panel in the door – Annie sitting up in the bed, with the tiny thing, wearing a onesie that Marion herself had sent, held uncertainly to her chest.

Marion paused outside the door, wanting to hold on to this moment of seeing them like that. She wiped a single surprising tear from her eye, and then a second. And then laughed for a moment, silently, at the fact that she was shedding tears.

Then she pushed the door open and went in. She was smiling.

Annie looked up and immediately said, almost shouted at her, 'He's blind.'

Marion just stood there.

'They say he's blind,' Annie said. 'That's what they say.'

Marion, stuck in the doorway, was half-aware of the fact that she was still smiling.

'That's what they say,' Annie said again.

Marion knew she couldn't just stand there. She had to do something.

She stepped to the bed and took the baby from her daughter. And it was as if she hadn't heard what Annie had said. She was just doing what she would have done if Annie hadn't said those things.

'Did you hear what I said?' Annie asked.

'Yes, I heard you.'

'And? Don't you have anything to say?'

Marion struggled. Finally she asked, 'Does Doug know?'

'Yes. As soon as they told him,' Annie said, in tears now, 'he left.'

'He left?'

'Yes – he left!'

Marion was staring at the hours-old thing in her hands, the red creases in the face that seemed to be made of red creases. The black feathers of hair on the tender skull. She had never warmed to newborns – even Annie had seemed ugly to her when they handed her over. In fact she didn't like kids much at all. After Annie she had known she was done. She had had no desire to do it again, any of it.

She was staring at the baby's velvety skull and struggling again to think of something to say.

'Does he have a name?' she asked, finally.

'Thomas,' Annie said, with tears sliding down her face.

'That's nice.'

Supporting the baby's head, Marion sat carefully down on the chair that was there. He seemed weightless in her hands. She was very aware of her failure to be equal to the needs of this moment. That her daughter needed something from her was painfully evident. It was also painfully evident that she didn't seem to have what was needed – didn't even seem to know what it was.

'I like it,' she said, still talking about the name, though too much time had passed and it wasn't obvious what she meant. And anyway it seemed like a useless thing to say, a thing which simply emphasised the fact that she had no words that might actually be able to help.

She felt her own failure as a human being, and more than anything she just wanted to leave – and then she felt that that desire to leave was also a kind of failure, and a shameful one, so that it was difficult even to look Annie in the eye.

When she handed Thomas back to Annie, she asked, in a way that still failed to acknowledge what she had been told, if there was anything that Annie needed. And yes, there were some things. Marion, taking her pen out of her hand-bag, wrote a neat list.

She wandered the aisles of the supermarket in a daze. She already knew that the significance of what had just happened would expand as time passed – would expand, in her own mind, and in Annie's too, into something huge, into a major failure, of motherhood, of humanity. It would become a defining event in their lives, from which neither of them would ever be entirely able to escape, whatever happened in the future.

It was one of those events, she thought, that make us what we are, for ourselves and for other people. They just seem to happen, and then they're there forever, and slowly we understand that we're stuck with them, that nothing will ever be the same again.

When someone said her name she did not, for a few seconds, understand that they were talking to her. Two women were standing there. They looked Chinese or something. The younger of the two was smiling at her.

'Excuse me,' she said again. 'Are you Marion Mackenzie, the writer?'

Marion had to think about it, she had to take

a moment to ask herself whether she was in fact 'Marion Mackenzie, the writer'.

'Yes,' she said. 'I am.'

'I'm such a huge fan of yours,' the woman said.

'Thank you,' Marion said.

'My name's Wendy.'

'Nice to meet you, Wendy.'

'Are you okay? You seem very wet,' Wendy said, the smile vanishing from her face.

Marion was indeed very wet – she was dripping onto the floor and her hair was stuck to her forehead. She had walked for ten minutes through a downpour to get to the supermarket.

'Yes, I'm fine,' she said. 'I need to buy an umbrella,' she added, trying to make light of it.

'Yes, you need one here,' Wendy said. And then, 'This is my mom, Jackie.'

At the sound of her name, the older woman just nodded. She was about Marion's age.

'Hello,' Marion said to her tentatively, wondering if she even spoke English.

'She's over from Hong Kong,' Wendy said. 'She teaches English Lit in college there.'

'Oh.' Marion tried to seem unsurprised, and interested. 'Okay.'

'She teaches your work actually.'

'Oh yeah? Well. That's . . . very nice . . .'

Marion again looked at the older woman, Jackie, who again merely nodded, and smiled.

Then Wendy said, 'Well it was such a pleasure to meet you.'

'You too.'

It seemed, at that point, that the encounter was at an end. Wendy, though, had another question – 'What are you doing in Seattle?'

'I'm, uh. I'm here to visit my daughter,' Marion said, touching her hair, and finding herself momentarily shocked at how wet it was.

'She lives here?'

'Yes, she does.'

'Okay,' Wendy said, full of enthusiasm. 'Would you mind,' she asked, 'I know you must get this all the time, would you mind signing something for me?' She had her handbag open and was trying to find something, some piece of paper, for Marion to sign.

'Sure,' Marion said.

Wendy laughed. 'I wish I had one of your books with me.' She handed Marion instead a small notebook, and a pen.

Marion wrote her name on the open page of the notebook, and handed the things back.

'Thank you so much,' Wendy said.

'Sure.'

'You're a wonderful writer.'

'Thank you,' Marion said, and to Wendy's surprise, she soggily embraced her.

'Oh!' Wendy said. 'Wow!'

Marion, in fact, was very emotional suddenly. With tears in her eyes, she simply nodded at the older woman, Jackie, who taught her work to students in Hong Kong, and then turned and hurried away down the supermarket aisle.

Filsan

by Nadifa Mohamed

1.

Filsan rises and takes her uniform from the peg on the door. She pulls her tunic over her head and her trousers over her legs. A quick visit to the bathroom and then she is beside the stove in the communal kitchen, the wall above her blackened with soot, the smell of food still in the air from the previous night. Water boils in her saucepan, tea leaves, cardamom pods and cloves shivering on the surface of it. As it's about to bubble over, she grabs the handle and pours just enough to fill her enamel cup.

She drinks the tea immediately, its heat scorching her throat in a way she finds pleasant. This is all she has for breakfast. Back home, her housekeeper Intisaar would have covered the dining table with a vinyl sheet decorated with small yellow flowers and laid out a flask of black tea, a jug of orange juice, a fruit salad of mangoes, papayas and bananas, flatbreads and, if her father had requested it the night before, scrambled eggs and lamb kidneys.

The other women – there are about fifty altogether in the barracks – drift into the kitchen while Filsan gazes at the view beyond the window: a bare yard criss-crossed by poles and clothes lines with the two domes of the central mosque on the horizon. She ignores her comrades as they ignore her, but what would she say to them if she could? She would tell them that she has never been good at making friends, that her housekeeper Intisaar's children had seemed kind but hadn't been allowed inside the house by her father, that the neighbourhood kids had scorned her, that she found it easier to talk to her father's friends.

Filsan rinses her cup, locks it away and returns to her room to make the bed before departing for the offices of the Mobile Military Court. She hears laughter from the kitchen as she turns the handle to her door, and knows it is aimed at her. As she enters she finds herself overwhelmed by an urge to cry out with anger that her life should be so small and unimportant, that this two-metre-by-two-metre cell that is her room should be the span of her world.

The brick chimney of the offices of the Mobile Military Court jutting out from one of the rooftops is something Filsan had never seen in Mogadishu, where the weather was never less than sultry, but here the wind can be cold and fierce. In her office there are just two desks, one for Captain Yasin and a small, scratched one for her, Corporal Adan Ali.

She is an office worker, neither noticed nor appreciated by the uniformed men above her. Despite two years of enlistment in the Women's Auxiliary Corps and five years before she came here working for the Victory Pioneers in Mogadishu, her chief tasks are still those of a secretary.

Had her father been dreaming or lying when he told her that she would make the ground shake here in Hargeisa? Had he been drunk? Or just desperate to remove her from Mogadishu to protect her? If she had to create a file on her own father where would she even begin? He had shown her both tenderness and contempt, cruelty and honour. She remembers him now pacing the flat roof of their three-storey villa in Mogadishu, a strip of the Indian Ocean visible between two slender minarets, watching over the neighbourhood with binoculars, scanning east and west for the spies he believes watch him.

Captain Yasin arrives, tall and elegant in his black beret.

Filsan stands up and salutes him but he waves her back to her chair.

'Now don't get too excited, Miss Corporal, but I spoke to Major Adow a few days ago and he asked me if I could recommend someone to go on a mission to the border. I looked high and low and then I remembered you, crouched over your little desk. Such efficiency! Such honesty!'

Filsan looks up at him, with half contempt, half desire.

'To Birjeeh with you, on the double!' He points dramatically to the door and she laughs despite herself. As she leaves the room, his eyes track her with an interest she doesn't find unwelcome.

Birjeeh Military HQ reminds Filsan of an illustration in one of the fairy-tale books she read as a child. Like an enchanted castle, it is perched on a hill, partially hidden behind high walls with watchtowers. The concrete armoury now functions as a detention room and she can imagine long-forgotten prisoners with scraggly beards hidden in secret, underground cells.

The logistics officer, Lieutenant Hashi, ushers her to the Major's office with a scowl on his tight, fox-like face.

The room is crowded with around thirty bulky commandos from the local 26th Infantry Division. They stand in a crescent shape around Major Adow.

'Come closer, comrades,' he says before standing up.

Lieutenant Hashi unrolls a map on the table and then pins its corners to the felt board behind the desk. It shows the north-western region of Somalia in minute detail: waterholes, reservoirs, dry riverbeds, dirt tracks. There are three blue circles on the map over villages near the Ethiopian border; enclosing the blue circles are red semicircles.

Major Adow points his pen at each blue circle and names it in turn.

'Salahley, Baha Dhamal, Ina Guuhaa. We have solid intelligence that NFM rebels are fed, watered and sheltered in these villages. They have become bolder and bolder and it is places like these villages that allow them to think they stand a chance in hell of defeating us.'

Filsan stands at armpit height to the soldiers. She finds herself enjoying their smell, the musk of their sweat mixed with hair and gun oil.

'You are charged with demolishing the water reservoirs of Salahley. They have been building one every year for more than ten years now and have given some over to the rebels to use. Corporal Adan Ali! Where are you, my girl?' Major Adow shouts.

Filsan pushes forward.

'It is your duty to inform the villagers of our anger. They must understand that further punishment can and will be enforced. We need an educated comrade who can clearly state to them the principles of our revolution. That's you, isn't it?'

'Yes, Major,' Filsan replies quickly.

'Inform them they will have water trucked in monthly and they can use their traditional wells.'

'I will tell them, sir.'

'The exact date and time of the operation will be confirmed by Lieutenant Hashi. Are there any questions?'

The soldiers shift nervously but don't reply. Filsan clears her throat and all faces turn to her.

'Will we be taking prisoners?' she almost whispers.

Major Adow smiles broadly, the same kind of smile he would give a dog riding a bicycle. 'Good question, *jaalle*. We have yet to confirm that detail but well done for speaking up.'

The other soldiers smile condescendingly, even though they were too cowardly to raise their own voices.

2.

The call comes two days later.

The plan is to leave Hargeisa the next day at five in the morning and to arrive in Salahley by 7 a.m. Taking a deep breath she forces herself through her morning routine. She arrives at Birjeeh before the others, the sky still dark but birds flapping and shaking one another awake in the branches.

The unit of thirty men and Filsan leave Birjeeh in a convoy of four large trucks of the type the locals called 'the fates' because of their role in dozens of fatal traffic accidents. Filsan rides in the passenger seat of the first truck.

'Morning, Corporal.' Lieutenant Afrah twists his neck into the cab from the bench behind.

'Good morning, sir.' Filsan salutes awkwardly. The Lieutenant has the strange-coloured eyes that some Somalis possess, brown around the pupil with a thick halo of blue as if he is going blind.

'Are you nervous?' He smiles and reveals the sweet gap between his teeth.

'No, I just want to do a decent job.'

'It will be easy, in and out before the engine's even cooled. I have a rifle here for you, an FAL automatic. The recoil isn't so bad on them, better for you than the Kalashnikov. In any case, Major Adow said you have had arms training?'

'With the Women's Auxiliary Corps, but that was some time ago, I don't know . . .'

'You won't need it. It will just be a deterrence in case there are any troublemakers in the village.'

'Yes, Lieutenant.' Filsan takes the weapon from him; the stock is relatively short while the barrel scrapes the roof of the lorry. She holds it across her chest with the strap over her back. She had never hit the targets well during practice in Mogadishu but it feels good to hold a rifle again; a gun makes a soldier even out of a woman.

They pass the last checkpoint and leave the messy, compact town to disappear in the rearview mirror. A rim of light is developing all around them, like overexposed film, the horizon broken up by lopsided pyramids of granite. It is a barren landscape, as strange to her as any foreign country.

There are no signs or obvious landmarks; the driver seems to know instinctively which forks in the road to take.

Filsan asks how nomads navigate on moonless nights in these desolate areas, and the driver points up to the sky. 'Maybe God tells them or they still know the old maps of the stars and find their way like that.'

Her own ancestors weren't wanderers but quietly acquired land and wealth. Here, this wild terrain seems to have shaped the character of the people.

As the lorry approaches the border with Ethiopia it begins to climb slowly but steadily, the air fresh and scented by the yellow flowers of gum arabic trees. A young shepherd hides behind a thicket of acacia as the convoy passes, his small figure just visible between the scrubby crowns, his black-headed sheep grazing across a vast distance.

When they arrive at Salahley, it is barely even a village. There are a few beehive-shaped dwellings with old cloth hanging from their entrances, a tea shop with kettles resting on open fires, one solitary stone building with a tin roof, goats, stray children, and a cleared space under a tall tree for religious lessons and clan meetings.

The elders have been summoned and Filsan remembers her role. She steps forward to intercept the three men but they ignore her, and carry on with their sticks and bandy legs as if to speak to a young soldier behind her.

She grabs the man on the right by the arm, '*Jaalle*, it is me you need to speak with.'

He is a thin, wiry man but he shakes her off

with surprising force. Filsan pursues him, not willing to ask for anyone's assistance in dealing with him. She wants to drag him back by the long tufts of grey hair around his bald head and make him kneel at her feet. She catches up with him and shoves the barrel of her gun in the small of his back. 'Stop!'

He freezes and turns slowly to face her.

She withdraws the rifle but holds it tightly, still aimed in his direction.

'My commander has instructed me to speak with you. We are here with the full authority of the government. There is strong evidence that you have been assisting the outlawed National Freedom Movement, and to prevent further collaboration the reservoirs surrounding this settlement will be destroyed.' Filsan speaks in a rush, not stopping to breathe. 'You may continue to use your traditional drop wells and will be supplied with additional water once a month by the local government.'

The whole village now seems to have crowded around her. The other soldiers have disappeared into the shacks.

'This is government land,' Filsan raises her voice and gestures to the expanse beyond them, 'and you do not even deny that you use the reservoirs to support the terrorists.'

The third elder, younger than the other two leaders, and still with a full head of black hair, joins the conversation.

'*Jaalle*,' he says mockingly to Filsan, 'we use those *berkeds* to water our camels, our goats and sheep, to wash before prayers, for a cup of tea in the mornings. We are in the middle of a long drought; do you think we would give water to rebels?'

And then a huge plume of water, mud and stone flies into the sky to the west of the village, the bellow of the dynamite destroying the reservoirs echoing against the limestone hills. The villagers run towards the explosions, the elders in the lead, children yelping in excitement and fear behind them.

Filsan catches up with the crowd just as Lieutenant Afrah orders the final detonation. The rectangular cement walls of the nearest reservoir are blown into fragments and fresh water glides over the parched, eroded earth and slips quietly into deep cracks on the surface.

The destruction silences the elders. Filsan can sense their anger in the same way she had learned to read her father's; the set of their jaws, the tension in their shoulders, their bodies angled away from the subject of their hate.

Then, the soldiers begin to appear, smiling

and relaxed, unconcerned by the reaction of the villagers. These kinds of raids are welcome to them, bringing little risk and potential loot. Filsan pants after her chase and presses her palm against the stitch in her ribs. The villagers are rooted to the soil, looking at the destroyed reservoirs, their heads turning from crater to crater, false rain dripping from the acacias.

She marches towards the elders, planning to explain once again why they acted as they did, and the benefits the villagers could enjoy if they only shunned the rebels.

As she approaches them, the red-haired elder swivels and swings his cane at her face. She doesn't even notice her finger squeeze the trigger of her rifle as her whole body recoils from the gunshots. The knock of the rifle against her chest surprises her as does the sudden pop of bullets. When the elder falls back onto his behind she thinks he has lost his balance trying to strike her, until points of blood spring up over his shirt, turning the white cloth a red that darkens before her eyes. Then, strangely, the two other elders decide to drop to the ground too, their open eyes still watching her as they fall wounded.

'Hold fire!' shouts Lieutenant Afrah.

Filsan looks down at her feet and sees bronzed beetles scuttling over them. She presses one boot on the other, and the beetles are stilled, transformed into empty bullet shells.

The elders are slumped over each other like drunks; Filsan hears a howl as first one woman and then another and then another rushes towards the dying men.

Filsan tries to move but her boots feel like cement.

Lieutenant Afrah aims his Kalashnikov at the young men in the crowd. 'Get back! Back! Back!'

A group of soldiers force them back. Filsan notices for the first time how thin their calves are, just shafts of bone. They are hustled away, hands on the back of their afros, to squat in the sun until the soldiers depart.

An old woman pulls the wives off the corpses and shrouds the men's faces under a shawl. She says nothing but turns to Filsan and points a finger; whether it is to lay blame, mark her out for revenge or curse her, Filsan cannot tell.

'Get in the truck, *jaalle*,' Lieutenant Afrah orders.

Filsan peers down at her distant boots. 'But I can't move.'

Afrah clicks his fingers and a conscript no older than fifteen comes to his side. 'Escort her back to the truck.'

The conscript takes her elbow gently, like he

would with his grandmother, and leads her forward as she stumbles over the broken ground.

'You did well, *jaalle*,' he keeps repeating in her ear, as they trek the half-mile back to the vehicles.

'But what happened? Who killed them?' she whispers.

3.

Filsan smoothes her palms over her wooden desk, enjoying its solidity; she closes her eyes and can still see in her mind the dying elders looking back at her. She filed their deaths as accidental and was advised to have their older sons detained. It's not guilt that she feels thinking about them but more a sense of unease.

Captain Yasin makes an aeroplane from a card and throws it at her desk; it glides just short and lands beside her feet. It is her request for leave stamped with 'approved'. Filsan will soon be back in her yellow room at home with the cherry-print curtains. She craves Intisaar's cooking, her crispy lamb *sambuusi*, the grilled fish served with spiced and sweetened vermicelli, and hot oily *bajiye* dipped in green chilli sauce.

Filsan opens a window to clear the room of

the captain's cigarette smoke and stands idly for a moment watching the wind shake desiccated leaves into the yard.

'You want to come to Saba'ad with me before you go on leave?' Captain Yasin's voice startles her. 'I'm going to check on the militia we are training there for my report.'

The report *I* will end up writing, thinks Filsan as she sinks into her chair.

'What about these files?'

'They're not going to walk away, are they?' He pulls her up from her chair. 'Come on. It is an order.'

Filsan scribbles a note on her desk with her whereabouts and follows him to the jeep.

Saba'ad is twenty miles north-east of Hargeisa. It is the largest of five refugee camps in the north-western region, and stretches as far as the eye can see. Twenty thousand Ethiopian Somali refugees scratch out a living here, having first fled the fighting between '77 and '78 and then the subsequent famines in eastern Ethiopia.

The camp's residents live in a mishmash of dwellings scrabbled together from donated tarpaulin, acacia twigs, old cloth and scavenged metal. At different points of the camp, various charities run schools, clinics, community centres.

Filsan covers her nose and eyes against the gusts of sand and dust and keeps close to Captain Yasin. They arrive at the burial ground to the west of the camp where the men are waiting, around fifty or so, squatting between the rocks placed to mark graves. The fighters are ragged teenagers armed with long sticks and wear sandals made of tyre rubber. They rise as Captain Yasin and Filsan climb towards them.

'Is this all of you?' Captain Yasin asks.

Their leader is tall and skeletal; a green cap obscures his eyes. 'No, we have more but they are tending what animals they still have.' His voice is grainy, dry.

'This is Corporal Adan Ali, she will be working with you too.'

They squint in Filsan's direction.

'We need to know how many of you there are before we can arrange proper arms,' says Yasin.

'When we have our weapons then we will come out into the open. Not before.'

The leader scrapes pictures into the grit as he speaks; straight lines, suns, hills, curved horns. 'We are waiting for the signal.'

'It won't be long now. You must gather as many men as possible. Organise them. Discipline them,' Captain Yasin exhorts.

'What will you give us for the time being?' the leader asks.

The teenagers lean forward to hear the response.

'We will set aside more rations for you but there is little we can do until we take control of the city.'

Filsan looks up quizzically.

The leader nods, defeated. 'We will just wait, then.'

'Don't despair. Soon your fortunes will change for the better. Within the month you will have rifles, RPGs, transport. This girl will make sure of that.' He gestures at Filsan.

She doesn't understand. Why would they give weapons to these refugees when Somalia already has one of the largest armies in Africa? She wonders if he has drawn her into weapon smuggling.

She leaves and traces the route back to the jeep. Captain Yasin is soon beside her but she ignores him.

'What's wrong?' He pulls her arm back.

'Let me go!' She wrenches it free, not caring that he is her superior.

'Wait, Filsan! What's the problem?'

'I will report you, Captain. Commit as many crimes as you want, but don't drag me down with you.'

'What crimes?'

'Don't think I'm stupid. I may be a woman but I can't be fooled so easily.'

'What are you talking about?'

Filsan stops abruptly and lowers her voice. 'You are selling arms.'

He bends back with laughter. 'You're crazy! Selling arms? To them? And what would they pay me in?'

'So why tell them they will receive rocket-propelled grenades?'

He pulls her close. 'Because that is what the government wants. We can't talk about this here.' He takes her arm again and marches her to the car.

'Get in the jeep,' he orders. 'I can't tell you everything but I will tell you what I know.'

They drive away from Saba'ad in silence. Only when they have reached the long, empty road to Hargeisa does Captain Yasin feel comfortable talking.

'The government has decided that the situation as it stands can't continue. If the NFM rebels continue to attack a village here, a battalion there, other local militias will gain in confidence. Soon we will be fighting on twenty fronts.

'The leadership have decided that the whole population must be moved to prevent the terrorists taking over.'

'Empty Hargeisa?'

'All the towns, Hargeisa, Burao, Berbera, anywhere the rebels might gather.' He wipes sweat from his upper lip with his wrist.

'When will this happen?'

'Not confirmed.'

It seems sensible, final, an improvement on this constant, draining game.

'How do you know about it?'

Captain Yasin smiles. 'Ahh, don't you know that I am in the inner circle?'

'When will the rest of us be told?'

'Only when it is absolutely necessary. Filsan, please, you cannot tell anyone about this, or we will both end up in jail.' He holds her gaze in the rear-view mirror.

'Don't insult me. I am not some market gossip. I take my work more seriously than anyone else.'

He nods. 'That's why I told you.'

4.

The next day, as evening approaches, Yasin asks what she plans to do with her night.

'Read, Captain.'

'Poor girl, is that the extent of your existence?'

Filsan sits rigidly. 'I am not here for fun. I want to make something of myself.'

'Life is to be enjoyed.'

'For layabouts and street boys, maybe.'

'No, for you and for me too. Let me take you out to dinner.'

Filsan's eyes sweep down to her hands. 'I don't know.'

'Are your books really more interesting than me?'

'I have work to do.'

'As do I. Let's discuss it over a meal.'

Captain Yasin waits under an electricity pole a hundred yards from the barracks. He appears thin and angular in a white shirt that glows in the dim light. Filsan has changed into a pair of flared jeans and a loose red tunic with a shawl over her shoulders. They meet awkwardly and shake hands under the light of a nearby tea stall, her hand tiny in his.

'Captain Yasin, pleased to meet you.' He hides his grin.

'Filsan, likewise.'

Walking beside him, Filsan feels a static charge as if the cables above are lightly electrifying them; it surprises her how good it feels to stand beside a man and know that he has picked her from all of the other women he could have.

Yasin leads the way with his hands in his pockets and makes small talk about the restaurants he likes, the hotels that serve alcohol, the best places to meet senior officials.

They turn right at a checkpoint, and enter the Safari, an open-air restaurant with tame wildlife roaming the grounds.

It is packed with men in uniform, seated on white plastic chairs around tables set unevenly into the gravel beneath. Red lightbulbs hang in a chain from one corner to the next and the drone of a generator masks the music from two large speakers.

The men glance up from their card games and meals to judge the woman in their midst.

'Is this OK?' Yasin asks, pointing to a dark table under a bougainvillea bush.

Filsan knows what the stares mean. That she is a whore to be seen in public with a man she isn't married to. Their eyes are still on her as she slips into the chair. A waiter appears quickly beside Yasin.

He orders two colas and a lamb platter.

Slowly attention drifts away from Filsan back to the red heart of the restaurant.

'*Bedus*.' Yasin smiles. 'You would think they have never seen a woman before.'

'Uneducated, that is all.'

'Or jealous.' He strokes her little finger with his knuckle.

'Don't do that.' Filsan snatches her hands from his reach.

He raises his palms submitting to her request.

'Why are you not married already?' he asks

'No one has wanted me.'

'Do you know the reason why?'

'No, why?' Filsan smiles with surprise. She decides to be blunt.

'Because you act like you don't need anybody,' he continues.

'I *don't* need anyone but that doesn't mean that I don't want certain things.'

'And those certain things are?'

'Someone by my side, on my side, who I can share my thoughts with.'

Yasin lights a cigarette, adding another pin-prick of light to the dark. 'Thoughts about the organisational budget of our office, or other thoughts?'

'All kinds. You wouldn't guess how far and deep my thoughts reach.'

'*Ahh*, so you are philosophising up there in your little bedroom.'

The waiter returns with a tray piled high with rice and a lamb shoulder and two cola bottles rough with reuse.

'Sometimes. At other times I am just wishing something good would happen in my life.'

'Something like me?'

Filsan raises an eyebrow. 'That is very arrogant.'

'Maybe, but is it wrong?'

'I don't know yet. Why have you suddenly become so attentive?'

'Time. We have much less time than we realise, especially as soldiers, and I don't want to wait for anything.'

Filsan lifts the bottle to her mouth to hide her smile. 'That is very dramatic but our office is pretty safe, isn't it?'

'For now. But don't worry, you have me to protect you.'

'I think *I* would be better at protecting you.'

Yasin walks Filsan back to the barracks. The street is dark and deserted because of the civilian curfew, apart from the squeak and rustle of stray cats chasing mice and the soldiers at the checkpoint talking softly over the hiss of a radio. The sky stretched over them like a dome is alive with stars; thin black clouds with haloes of white and silver pass over the half-moon.

'You know that on clear nights you can spot satellites?' Yasin says.

'I've heard that. In Mogadishu there are too many lights to see anything like this.' Filsan carries on staring at the heavens and stumbles over a stone.

Yasin catches her by the waist; for a moment her hands rest on his and then she pushes them away.

They stroll slowly to the barracks.

'You should stop here in case anyone sees you,' Filsan says, turning to him and holding out her hand. 'See you tomorrow.'

Yasin chuckles at her formality but shakes her hand.

He waits for her to pass the sentry gate and enter the compound. Out of sight in the stairwell, Filsan watches him turn and walk away. She feels a pang in her chest as he strides, head bowed, into the dark. He seems so vulnerable, prey to whatever ghosts or beasts might find him. Filsan begins to blow a kiss at his back but feels ridiculous and just follows his white shirt as it disappears into the night like a ship's sail surrounded by high waves and low clouds.

No Need to Fear the Depths

by Andrey Kurkov
translated by Elizabeth Sharp Kourkov

There are people among us who have an instinctive connection with their motherland which switches itself on at exactly the same time every year. No, I'm not talking about a country or a state. I mean the particular patch of soil on which someone is born.

Not long ago, I met just such a person. We were brought together by the jazz festival in Koktebel, on the Crimean Peninsula. As soon as he realised I was from Kiev he immediately started treating me as a friend and, I must say, I felt no desire to protest. We exchanged telephone numbers on parting and suddenly in mid-September I get a call.

'It's Nikolai here! It's my birthday on Saturday. You must come. No excuses! We'll leave from the tram stop on Shevchenko Square. Don't forget your swimming trunks!'

I looked out of the window. It had only just

stopped raining. There was no promise of warmth in the air. Perhaps he knows someone in a weather-related job, I thought, or maybe someone higher still! The one who makes the weather!

At ten o'clock on Saturday morning, as promised, I was at the tram stop. The sun really was shining. Only a few non-threatening clouds floated across the sky. But it wasn't hot.

I was expecting a barbecue picnic in pleasant company. Someone would probably bring a guitar and towards evening we would sit round a fire singing the popular songs of our youth. Nikolai and I were almost exactly the same age. It was his fifty-second birthday and I would celebrate mine in sixth months' time.

He drove up in a new, white Skoda. There was no one but him in the car.

'How many folk will there be?' I asked as we turned onto the road leading to the Kiev Sea – the name we give to a big lake near Kiev.

'About six. But the others are making their own way. They're not from Kiev.'

The city was left behind. Pine forest flashed by on either side of the road, interrupted only by the occasional plain-looking village.

'Did you bring your swimming trunks?' asked Nikolai.

'Yes, I did. Is the water still warm?'

'It's OK on the surface, but pretty chilly further down.'

Half an hour later we turned onto a dirt track that ran through forest and ended on the shore of the Kiev Sea. A motorboat had been pulled onto the sandy beach and standing beside it were two bearded men in camouflage overalls. They stood smoking in silence, but on seeing us they smiled. They hugged Nikolai and then greeted me respectfully, shaking my hand.

'Everything all right?' asked Nikolai.

'Fine.' One of them replied. 'Let's leave the food in the car, so as not to overload the boat.'

Nikolai nodded and they threw three large shopping bags into the Skoda's boot. One of which evidently contained glass bottles.

Nikolai locked the car and signalled to me to get into the boat.

Sitting in the bow, I watched the smooth, endless sheet of the water's surface, which our boat cut in two with ease and confidence. Then, I noticed, through the hum of the engine, a different, metallic sound. I turned round and saw Nikolai sitting at the helm while his friends busied themselves with two aqualungs which lay on the metal bottom of the boat.

Suddenly feeling uneasy, I looked back at

the water. It was greenish, thick, not at all transparent.

'We'll be there soon,' shouted Nikolai, apparently noticing my concern.

About five minutes later, one of the bearded men took over from Nikolai at the helm. We were moving slowly now and everyone, except me, was watching the water on one side of the boat.

'Turn her off!' Nikolai shouted suddenly. And at once the motor went dead.

He fitted two light oars in the rowlocks. Then, changing places with me, picked up the rope attached to the bow of the boat.

'Left a bit!' he commanded.

One of his friends took up the oars and carried out Nikolai's instructions.

'Stop!' shouted Nikolai.

I looked around. The only land in sight was the beach on which we had left the car. In all other directions there was nothing but water.

About two metres away from the boat, a metal pin stuck out about ten centimetres above the water. When the boat was close enough, Nikolai tied the rope round the pin and, turning to his bearded friends, asked:

'Is everything ready?'

Both nodded.

'Have you done any diving?' he asked me.

'A long time ago,' I replied a bit confused. 'Where are we going?'

'To my motherland.'

Alarmed, I looked again at the smooth watery surface. Now it looked cleaner, more transparent. I turned back to the metal pin to which the boat was fastened and realised that it was the top of a church's cross.

At that moment, Nikolai's mobile rang.

'Hi there,' he said to the caller. 'You've arrived? Park next to my Skoda and make up a fire. We'll be there in about two hours.'

Then he took off his clothes, pulled on a wetsuit and arranged his aqualung on his back, glancing at me from time to time as if to say: 'Hurry up then!'

I struggled into a wetsuit.

'I was christened in that church below the surface,' said Nikolai, nodding towards the top of the cross. 'And I was born about a hundred metres away. Let's go.'

The bearded men handed us each a powerful underwater torch. Nikolai perched momentarily on the side of the boat with his back to the water before pushing himself off. I followed.

The wetsuit really did keep out the cold. As I swam downwards, rays of sunlight pierced the water's surface and lit up the yellowish dome and white walls of the church. A few minutes later I noticed some brick houses even further down. Nikolai tapped me on the shoulder and shone the beam of his torch towards the house which was furthest from us. We made for that one.

There were no doors on the underwater house. Having swum to the doorway, Nikolai shone his torch inside. We could see the remains of a brick stove. Nikolai indicated that I should stay there and he went in alone. He was gone for several minutes and I began to worry. I shone my torch into the house, but could not see him. Eventually he returned. Through the glass of his mask I could see he had been crying. He waved his arm in a 'follow me' gesture.

Some two hundred metres further along we found ourselves above a village graveyard. We swam down to a double grave, adorned with two metal crosses, both of which were leaning sideways. Underwater we couldn't speak, but there was no need for words. I helped him to straighten the two crosses and then Nikolai pointed upwards with his index finger: 'Let's surface.'

We scrambled back into the boat and threw off our aqualungs. Our bearded companions gave us each a small glass of vodka to warm ourselves and while we got warm, the two of them put on the aqualungs and, without donning any wet suits, threw themselves backwards over the side of the boat.

'Where are they going? Were they born here too?' I asked Nikolai.

The birthday boy was clearly not in a celebratory mood.

'No, not here,' he sighed, ignoring my first question.

I was suddenly shot through with a sense of panic. My heart ached. My whole body seemed to be shaking with fear. I looked at the water and, to my amazement, the surface which, only a moment ago, had been so smooth was now shaking. This was not the usual circular motion of water disturbed, but more like the movement of volcanic lava. I could also hear a low hum in the air.

I looked up at the sky and then over towards Nikolai sitting in his underpants, cradling a glass of vodka in his hands. His expression, as before, was one of great sadness.

'There's something wrong,' I said, pointing to the strange movement of the water.

'There was something wrong forty years ago when those Soviet idiots saw fit to make a lake here,' he said, his voice cold and distant. 'They drowned hundreds of villages: the graveyards and churches, even the monuments to the "unknown soldier"! And now in order to pay my respects to my relatives, I must dive twenty metres underwater . . .'

'It looks like there'll be a storm,' I urged, interrupting him.

'Get closer to the water and listen carefully,' said Nikolai, in a friendlier tone.

I leaned over the side and put my ear almost to the surface of the water. Now the low humming sound was very clear.

'That's the lads ringing the bell,' he explained. 'They'll ring it fifty-two times. In honour of my birthday!'

I had never heard the sound of a bell rung under water. And it was not so much what I heard as what I saw. The strange shaking of the water above the drowned village; I will remember that for the rest of my days.

Nobody spoke as we travelled back to the shore. I found the silence annoying. It oppressed me.

'Where are you from?' I asked the bearded men, who, it turned out were brothers: Vassilii and Ivan.

'We were luckier than Nikolai,' replied Ivan on behalf of both. 'We were born three kilometres from Chernobyl, on a little farmstead. Even after the nuclear explosion all those years ago, the Geiger counters still scream like mad with all the radiation there, but we go twice a year. We have special protective suits for the "Zone".'

He went on. 'It's better there than underwater. At least you can go into your old home, sit down at your parents' table and drink a glass of vodka to their memory.'

We were now approaching the shore and I could already see Nikolai's white Skoda with his friends' Lada parked next to it. His other friends were sat round the camp fire.

The sun was still shining. The air had warmed up and it occurred to me that, after some barbecued meat and vodka, it would be quite reasonable to go for a swim in this man-made Kiev Sea and then sing a few songs in pleasant company. That is what I really wanted.

But another thought struck me. Perhaps, on our way, we had sailed over another drowned village, or, to put it more simply, over the drowned past of our one-time motherland. You cannot return to that past unless you really want to, unless you put on the aqualung and dive. Perhaps there's no need to go back. It is enough just to remember, once a year. To ring the bell, that no one but you will hear. Your bell. The one deep inside your soul.

Into the Mud

by Yael van der Wouden

Miryam wants to show me something down by a lake, so I go. Her bike got stolen, she says, and could I ride her there.

Miryam balances on the back of the bike, her hands on my waist. We're jostled with every bump, every pothole in the road, and she says, 'Watch *out*, Debby,' and I say nothing. We're allowed to be friends again now that school is out. Every summer, Miryam gets restless in the upstairs apartment – tired of the heat, tired of her parents' arguments. And so she heads downstairs and knocks on the door until Mum or I open it for her.

At last week's service, the rabbi spent forever talking about the evil spirit – the *dybbuk* they'd found hiding in some old man's microwave. Miryam came to sit next to me. 'You know Barbara Lessink saw the rabbi piss against a tree in the park last week. He was totally wasted.' She

86

laughed. Her breath smelled like bubblegum. Miryam was talking to me again. The seasons had changed.

From behind me on the bike, Miryam controls the journey: to the left at the roundabout, to the right after the bridge. We bike onward, until there are no more houses by the side of the narrow road, only weeds. Finally I say, 'I don't think bikes are allowed here.' Miryam digs her nails into my waist. 'God, you're such a pussy. Just *bike*.'

She guides us off the road, past waterways sunk into the grasses, past an empty field. Beyond that, there is a lake. Knotted willows lean out from the banks at an angle, as if they're falling. I have sweated circles into my shirt from the ride. Miryam tells me I look a mess, that I'd better take a swim, but the water is too murky for both of us.

She makes herself comfortable on the remains of a jetty, lights up a cigarette, lifts her head to the sun. When the wind wafts by, it carries the smoke, the scent of the almond oil she combs through her curls.

I say, 'Well?'

'Wait,' she replies, her eyes still closed.

I slouch next to her.

'Okay, I'll show you now,' she announces. She pulls me up, takes me to the lake's muddy edge.

But she lets go of my hand, kneels in the mud and gathers some of it into a mound. 'Watch,' she says.

To start with, it looks like nothing. The shaped mound looks dirty, like when we were kids and played in the mud, and had it stuck under our fingernails for days. Miryam was always messier than me. Even in childhood, she'd push her fingers into anything, breathless, thrilled. They'd come away oily, sticky, covered in muck. I'd hold my palms away from myself until we were home again and I could wash them clean.

She lights another cigarette. We're only fifteen and I wonder who buys these for her. Does she get them herself? Does she look as old to actual adults as she does to me?.

'You have to let him dry for a second,' she says.

'Let who dry?'

Her hands are covered in mud, all the way up to her elbows, and she's made – a shape. Sort of like a man.

'So, have you ever done this?' she asks, still smoking.

And I say, voice high, 'Done *what*?'

'Ah. You haven't.'

The day is blisteringly hot so the mud dries quickly. 'Cool,' she continues, then pulls out a pen and her pack of cigarettes from her pockets.

She tears off the lid. Unfolds it. Scribbles something on it and rolls it up. She stuffs the paper into the mud-man's ear. Then she's up on her knees, hovering over him. She digs a mouth with two fingers and spits into the hole.

'There.' She takes a few steps back. I take a step back.

The mud-man comes alive, making a sound like beads in a glass bowl. He has awkward, stumbling limbs, like a man who drank too much.

I say, 'Fuck,' and 'Fuck,' and take several more steps back.

'He won't do a thing, you know,' she says. 'Not unless I tell him.'

I watch him scramble around us. In her hurry, Miryam's made him short – he barely reaches my hip. She hasn't given him eyes, so he's lost. He has his arms out, and they slam into the trunks of the willows every time he turns. 'Keep going,' she says. He gets tangled in the branches.

'That's not what they're meant for, Miryam.' Even I know she's made a golem, a legendary creature.

She gives me a look. 'So you're a rabbi now, huh, Dvorah, you're a big smart rabbi?'

'I'm just saying . . .' I stop. I don't know what I'm saying.

We watch the golem fall and struggle to get

up. When he comes close, I jerk away. Miryam gets annoyed when I don't laugh.

'You're *boring*,' she says, and goes to the golem. She takes the paper from his ear and stomps him back into the ground.

On the bike ride home, she puts her face against the back of my shirt and says, 'That's why I don't hang out with you, because you're boring.' But she holds on very tightly, fists clutching the fabric over my navel. At our building, she runs ahead up the stairs and disappears to her floor without saying goodbye.

That night, in bed, all I can think of is the golem. Falling over itself, stumbling, trying to get up. And Miryam's smile, wavering at the edges.

One time last year at school, I was sitting alone at lunch.

Then Miryam showed up, followed by a group of other popular girls, less popular girls, girls who just wanted to be around her. She spoke at length about how the gym teacher who sent her out of class probably hated her because he probably was in love with her. *Pathetic*, she called him, and then suddenly everyone was talking about blowjobs. They kept saying that word, *blowjobs*, *blowjobs*, and then cackled. I tried very hard not to look. But it didn't work.

'Hey, Debby! Hey, Debby!' one of the group called over.

I glanced up. Then Miryam said, 'Do you know what a *blowjob* is, Debby?' And then, to her crowd: 'I don't think she knows what a blowjob is.'

I mumbled, 'I know what it is.'

Miryam stood up on the bench and said, 'What? What did you say? Oh my God, what did you say?' Her puffy jacket was sliding off her shoulders. She looked almost bare underneath it. The straps of her top were sliding down as well. It was so cold that day, but she wasn't shivering at all.

When we were younger, she'd sometimes sleep over. She'd clamber into my bed and I would worm legs-first into the sleeping bag meant for her. My bedroom was under Miryam's parents' bedroom and we'd often hear her parents shouting at each other.

Sometimes, she'd hold her head over the side of the bed and say, 'I'm not going to spit on you,' and then let a string of saliva fall slowly from her mouth. The game was: I wasn't allowed to move, and she'd see how long the string would get before sucking it back up. Once, it broke. The glob landed on my cheek. She gasped, then giggled until she'd worn herself out.

*

Tonight, Mum turns up the TV loud, hoping Miryam's parents hear it, get embarrassed, get quiet. If that doesn't work then she'll get ready to call the police. She's only had to twice, and it was terrible both times.

Mum says, 'Poor kid.' I go to the balcony and watch Miryam rush out of the building's front door, marching into the night with her head down. She stops to wipe a hand over her eyes, to light a cigarette.

She knows I'm watching her, and in that moment she looks up. Catches me.

I go back inside and put on my shoes. Mum asks where I'm going, and I tell her it's too hot inside. That I'm going for a walk. She misunderstands and says, 'They can't shout forever.' I say, 'I know.'

The sky is dark, and there are some boys around the side of the building letting a low-bass tune shudder out of a boombox. I bike through the neighbourhood and find Miryam in the park, with some older friends. They're sitting at a picnic table, passing around bottles. The orange streetlight makes the park look faded and colourless. Miryam is shiny, a sheen of sweat on her forehead.

I stand by a tree, bike still in hand, until they notice me. One of the guys says, 'Jesus, she scared the shit out of me,' and someone else says, 'Hey! What do you want?'

Miryam says, 'Oh, God, I know her.' She looks at me. 'Go home, weirdo.'

Then she says, 'Shoo! Shoo!' and gestures for me to scat. The group laughs.

I don't leave. I hold on to the handlebars. Miryam laughs loud and fake. 'What? What are you going to do? Are you going to sit with us? You going to get drunk, De-vo-rah?' She says making my full name sound stupid.

I don't know what to say. I'm not going to sit with them, and I'm not going to drink. Then Miryam gets up, finds a branch on the ground, and throws it – wobbly – in my direction. The branch grazes my leg and lands in the grass.

She flings out her hand. 'Be gone! Be goooone!'

I squeeze my handlebars once again. I hold her gaze.

She turns away and tells her friends: 'Sorry about her, oh my God.'

When I get home, the TV is off and Mum has gone to sleep. There is no sound from upstairs. I place one of my shoes between the door and the doorframe so that the door doesn't close all the way. I hope Miryam will come inside.

I go to bed.

I am asleep when Miryam comes back. I wake

up because it was silent and now it's not. My bedroom door opens and closes. I peer into the dark and see the shape of her moving vaguely. I think she's taking off her shirt, then her jeans.

I move over and she gets into bed with me. She smells of drink and smoke. Of almond oil and food made in a closed kitchen. She tucks her body into mine: her face into my neck, her arms around my middle. She breathes against my skin and holds on tight.

She doesn't say anything, but her breath is the shape of a word. I can't make out what the word is, but the skin of my throat has heard it, and the next word I will speak upon waking will be whatever she has put into me.

In the morning, Miryam is gone.

I go upstairs, and I knock on the door to Miryam's apartment. The hallway there smells like the dog who lives in the apartment opposite, and who is sometimes let out to piss in the corner by the stairwell. Miryam's dad answers the door. He's a reedy man with a mouth that goes too far up his cheeks, like someone stretched his lips when he was very young and they never went back to normal. 'Is Miryam home?' I ask.

Miryam is an unmoving bulk under her sheets. The room smells like earth.

I swallow. I open my mouth to say her name but don't. I sit on the side of the bed. I expect her to stir, to jerk awake. She doesn't. Her heartbeat was so slow and heavy in her sleep, last night. Her skin was so warm.

I take her arm and the blanket falls away. Her hand shoots up to cover her face. Her hair is matted down, wet from a shower.

I pull at her. She grunts and shifts away from me. A puff of dust flies up, settles. I grab her face in my hands. It's not her, yet it is, sort of. As if a sculptor had tried to recreate her from memory, and failed. Her nose is oddly shaped, the whites of her eyes tinged green. In the heat of the room, mud rolls down her cheeks, skin melting, reforming. I realise I'm looking at the golem. He looks at me like he, too, would rather not have participated.

I drop my hands, heart quick in my throat.

He sinks back into the bed. I ask him, 'Where is she?'

The golem says nothing.

I ask him again, 'Tell me where she went.' But he has no language, and no words to speak.

Back home, I tremble most of the day, nauseated, sitting on the balcony with my eyes fixed on the street below. Mum wonders if I have a fever. She fusses over how hot I am, but I say it's a hot day. I snap at her when she insists I come inside.

It's evening by the time the real Miryam is home again. I'm still on our balcony, and she's on hers; I look up and see her leaning over the rail.

She grins. 'Did you see him? It worked, didn't it? They thought it was me, they thought I was home all day. It totally worked.'

'That's not what they're meant for, Miryam,' I say, like before.

She sways back and forth on the railing. 'Whatever you say, Rabbi Dvorah.'

'He didn't look like you at all.'

'Whatever.' She stops swaying. 'It's not like my parents were going to check I was in my room anyway.'

We're on the fire escape when Miryam says she wants to go out. She's smoking and I'm sitting on the spiky metal step watching her. I inspect a grain of dirt on the metal and say, 'Go out with one of your friends.'

'I don't want to go out with my friends.' She puts her shoe on my bare knee. 'I want to go out with freaky Dvorah.'

'Don't call me that,' I say, but it comes out more like I'm *asking*, and she laughs and says, 'Sorry sorry sorry sorry sorry.' She says, 'If

I promise to never call you that again, will you go out with me, will you, will you, will you—!'

We get ready in my room. She rubs makeup on her face, and then does the same to mine. I look at myself in the mirror. I look like someone decided my outlines needed to be more bold, and now the lines were taking up most of my face. I tell her I want to wash it off.

'Nooo,' she says. 'I promise you, you look so good!'

I can't be sure this isn't another joke she's playing. But she holds my wrists, and won't let me wash my face, so I don't.

She makes me take her on the back of my bike again. A strip of my stomach is bare, and that's where she puts her hands. I say, 'We're not going to get in, they're never going to let us in.'

'They're one hundred percent going to let us in.'

She is right.

The bar we go to is buried in an alleyway off an alleyway. Everyone looks older than us, taller. Men with ponytails, straining in their jackets. A few girls up on a table.

Miryam makes me try a drink. I swallow it too quickly and it burns and I have to bend over, coughing. She smirks, but puts her hand on my back.

The next drink is sweeter. I say 'no' at first, and she says, 'Okay,' but she leaves it on the bar in front of me, and I drink it.

She says, 'Yeah, that one's better for you, huh.' She leaves me at the bar to dance with some guy. She's a good dancer, and he is not. He moves his hands around her body like he's drawing a line in the shape of a Coke bottle. Then, she is back, and next she is gone again. I am dancing, too, with her, but do not put my hands anywhere near where his hands were. Then she is gone again.

Someone is talking to me, his breath like Tic Tacs over beer. I say to him, 'I can't hear you.' This man is a stranger, who knows nothing about me, who doesn't even know my name. He puts his hand on the strip of my bare-belly skin and tries to move his hand up, and I say 'No!', shove him, and he shoves me back.

Miryam screams at him. She wasn't there before, but now she is. She pulls me away even though the guy holds on like a toothy-mouthed animal. Finally he gives up. 'Come *on*,' she says, dragging me along quickly.

In the bathroom, under the purple lights, she says, 'What did you tell him?'

'Nothing,' I say.

'Did you flirt with him?'

'I don't know,' I say. 'I don't think so?'

She leans back against one of the sinks. Her lipstick is a little smudged. She's breathing quickly. I don't know if she's angry or upset.

When she pushes off from the sink and comes at me, I take a step back. She hovers, for a moment. She's close enough that I feel her body heat, smell the drink on her breath.

The door swings open. Music from the club blares, and then the door swings closed again, muffles it. My tongue is stuck to the roof of my mouth.

Miryam says, 'Okay, fun night, whatever, I want to go home.'

But on the bike, when we get to the round-about, she says, 'Go right.'

I say, 'What's right?' and she says, 'Just do it.'

We pass by, old narrow buildings tilting to the side; the crumbling city wall, brown stone covered in moss and vines. The canals, the old fire station. Then the suburbs. The fields. The sky, at its furthest point, is the colour of white shocked into blue – and there's the freckle of a star on the horizon. When there are no more streetlights, we get off the bike and walk the rest of the way to the lake.

I lie down by the water and listen to it lap quietly near my head. Miryam makes a new golem, rolls up a piece of paper, fits it into his ear, and spits in his mouth. This time she makes him ride my bike, which he manages well enough. Eventually she gets bored with that, too, and comes to lie next to me.

My heart thumps, aches. She leans up on an elbow, looks down at me. She looks down at me for a while. She says, 'Your mascara is all fucked.'

I say, 'Okay.'

She kisses me. I open my mouth, I let her in. We make a sound like a hum. She puts her hand on my ribs, high on my ribs. We kiss for a long time. We kiss until my mouth is sore, and my stomach is a cavernous thing: three rocks left to tumble in a washing machine, going around and around and around.

Later, Miryam tells me about her boyfriend. He doesn't go to our school, she says. He's older, and he's at a different school. She shows me a passport photo of him that she keeps in her wallet. Sandy hair, gel. A few pimples next to his nose. She says, 'He's hot, isn't he hot?'

I shrug, and let her climb on top of me, and kiss me. Mum is in the other room, getting the table ready for Sabbath and Miryam's legs are between mine. In the apartment above, her mum is talking to her grandmother on the phone. Her laughter is a lot like Miryam's – a *ha ha ha!* that rolls from the throat, the shape of three quick waves.

Miryam sleeps over. Mum brings out the sleeping bag, says, 'Just like when you two were kids. So nice.'

When Mum leaves I have the sleeping bag in my hands, ready to lie on the floor, like usual.

But Miryam says, 'What the fuck are you doing? Get in here.' She moves and makes a space on the mattress. I feel clumsily big in my own body, but I get into bed next to her.

We kiss, briefly, and then she says – all in one breath, words wet against my mouth – 'Where would you go if you could go anywhere, where would you go?'

'I don't know,' I say. 'Where would you go?'

'As in, I could be there? As in, like, blink your eyes and you're there?'

It's her game, anyway, so I say, 'Sure.'

'A big hotel room,' she says. 'Or a swimming pool on the roof of a building. A desert. Or . . . like, it's here but there's no one else here. Like our whole building but all the people are gone. Like the whole city but all the people are gone.'

'No one left?' I ask. Her hand is tracing a path over my spine.

She says, 'No one.'

I say, 'What about me?'

'Okay,' she says. 'Okay, you can stay.'

She takes me to the park to meet her boyfriend. He's a skinny guy, too tall for his body. She wants me to like him, I can tell. She keeps on explaining him to me like a fun fact, even though he's right there.

Did you know that he's the school champion in short distance running?

Did you know he's super good on the guitar?

Did you know he can eat five hamburgers without throwing up?

When she says that I say, 'Gross.'

She's upset with me for the rest of the day. When we're back outside our apartment building, I say, 'Do you want to go somewhere?'

'No,' she says, but she won't go inside, either. She pulls leaves off a bush and tosses them down and says, 'Summer sucks here, everything's so boring!'

'Well, maybe your *boyfriend*'s boring.' It's the bravest thing I've ever said to her. The meanest, too.

She stills. 'What do *you* know about boyfriends?' She steps closer. Her voice has gone low. 'At least I have someone. At least I'm not—'

She doesn't finish. I swallow.

'You don't know anything, Debby,' she says.

'And you do?' I say it quietly. I am no longer brave.

'What do you want from me?' Miryam says. She means to sound annoyed, but this time I think she wants an answer. But I don't know what answer to give.

She blows out a short, scornful puff of air. 'Right. Okay. You know what?' And then she walks away.

That night, I suddenly wake up, cold and sweaty all at once. I can't make out the words from upstairs, but the voices are loud. From Miryam's father, a stream of accusations. Miryam's responses are cut off, smaller. Doors slam shut.

Then there are quick footsteps down the hallway, down the stairs. Miryam, cursing to herself. I hold my breath. Maybe she'll stop on our floor. Maybe she'll come to our door.

She doesn't. The footsteps continue down, until I can't hear anything anymore. I get out of bed, roll up a piece of notebook paper and wedge it between the door and the doorframe. I lie awake, and I wait, and finally I fall asleep.

The next day is quiet. I see my bike has been taken. That night, I once again leave a wedge in the door. But again she doesn't come.

The day after that, Miryam's dad knocks on our door in a way that panicked people do. Mum opens and he goes off: have we seen Miryam? She hasn't been home, have we seen her?

I go out onto the balcony and sit on the hot plastic chair. I take deep, deep breaths.

Fear sits low in my body.

When I get to it, the earth behind the apartment building is too hard for my purposes; the earth at the foot of the oak nearby too thin. There are too many eyes watching me in the park. So I end up in someone's backyard.

The windows of their house reflect the bright sky, and I can barely see inside, but the neighbourhood is quiet and no one is around. I think, *They're on vacation*, and dig into their flowerbed. Somewhere up in a tree, a blackbird is crying at nothing.

The earth is heavy. It soaks through my jeans when I kneel down. I can't be neat about what I'm doing. The dirt trails all the way up my arms. I realise it's harder than Miryam made it look to make the mud shapes hold together. But I manage all the same. Would Miryam be impressed if she were here? Would she go quiet at knowing that I, too, can make life out of dirt?

For the golem's eyes, I use two bottle caps

which I had in my pocket; Miryam found them at the lakeside last week, flattened and rusty, and thought they were pretty, 'in a sad, shitty way, you know,' and gave them to me as a joke. I kept them anyway. For the nose I use a button that came off Miryam's shirt one day without her noticing. I kept that, too.

My fingers shake when I write the truth on a piece of paper and slip it into the hole of its ear. I hold my spit over its mouth. I let it drip down.

I feel it when he comes alive. My heart, in something else's body. I feel the beat of it, double. I feel the air on my skin, double. I can taste the inside of my mouth, like mud.

I lean toward the golem and put my hands on him. 'Where?' I say it like an exclamation mark.

Gently, easily, he undoes my hold on him. He shifts like he is sighing, but he has no lungs, and no throat. He sits upright, turns, and gestures to his back. An invitation.

I have read the stories. I have listened when the rabbi spoke. I know, I know that this isn't what golems are meant for. I know about using good matter for bad ends, about evils close to home, about the wickedness of those who control living things and dead things.

I climb onto his back. He is damp sand under

my fingernails. Underneath, he is solid. He flies straight up. The city wobbles below us. At first I close my eyes, but then the thrill overtakes me and I open them. Everything below me is very small, and fits together so neatly. The cars all in a line on the road like children's toys.

I feel fear and power all at once. I know this feeling from hot afternoons with Miryam hovering over me, face close; first I am terrified, and then I *want*.

When we land, it's at the lake.

I see Miryam sitting on the bank. Her feet are in the water. I come down from the golem's back, and stagger on the firm ground.

She looks at my mud-covered clothes. She sees the golem, too. The corner of her mouth twitches at this.

She beckons the golem over, and he moves towards her. I feel his need to do as she wishes.

When he bends to her, he does so like a knight: on one knee, head down.

I watch as she kisses the crown of his head, and feel the echo on my skin. I watch as she takes the paper from his ear. I watch, too, as he dissolves. The earth tumbles into the reeds, and the wind carries the sand, and then it is gone.

I say, 'You took my bike.'

She shrugs. 'Well, yeah.'

I want to touch her. I sit down. She watches me with one eye shut against the glare of the sinking sun.

'So you've figured out how to make one, huh?' Then she adds: 'I made mine fly me into an empty hotel room. I can stay wherever I want to stay.' She swallows. 'Go wherever. Anywhere I tell him to.'

She still has the paper in her hands. If I look away, she might call him back again. If I look away, she might disappear. She lifts the paper until it's level with her face, until I have no choice but to look her in the eye. She says, 'Would you do anything I tell you to do?'

I say, 'Yes.'

'Will you leave me?'

I don't answer.

'Will you go if I tell you to?'

I take a breath.

She says, 'Shoo.'

She smiles, but it's not really a smile. It turns down at the corners. She takes a breath, then, and crinkles the paper to my ear, and kisses me. 'Shoo,' she says. 'Go. Be gone.'

She waits to see if I will do as commanded.

I wait, too. Water laps against the shore, insects shift in the reeds, the knotted willows bow, but I – a human being, a living person – I stay.

The Booker Prize Foundation is a registered charity designed to inspire more people to read – and write – the world's best fiction: because if you can imagine a different world, you can create a better one.

There are three Booker Prizes: the Booker Prize, the International Booker Prize and the Children's Booker Prize. Through them and other projects, the Foundation's aim is to become a partner for life: engaging new and existing readers from childhood onwards.

For decades, the Booker Prize Foundation has increased access to Bocker Prize titles through libraries, schools, universities and prisons, and among the partially sighted.

Working together, the Reading Agency and the Booker Prize Foundation hope to create a new library of Quick Reads by Booker Prize authors. These may lead readers to other books by those writers, to other Quick Reads, or they may form a way into the reading habit more generally.

thebookerprizes.com @TheBookerPrizes #BookerPrize

About Quick Reads

"Reading is such an important building block for success"

— Jojo Moyes

Quick Reads are short books written by bestselling authors.

Did you enjoy this Quick Read?

Tell us what you thought by filling in
our short survey. Scan the QR code
to go directly to the survey or visit:
bit.ly/QuickReads2026

Thank you to Penguin Random House, Hachette and all our publishing partners for their ongoing support.

A big thank you to Curtis Brown for supporting the 20th anniversary of Quick Reads.

A special thank you to Jojo Moyes for her generous donation in 2020–2022 which helped to build the future of Quick Reads.

Quick Reads is delivered by The Reading Agency, a UK charity that inspires social and personal change through the proven power of reading.

readingagency.org.uk @readingagency #QuickReads

The Reading Agency, Registered number: 3904882 (England & Wales)
Registered charity number: 1085443 (England & Wales)
Registered Office: 24 Bedford Row, London, WC1R 4EH
The Reading Agency is supported using public funding by
Arts Council England.

Quick Reads are available to buy in paperback or ebook
and to borrow from your local library. For a complete list of
titles and more information on the authors and their books visit:
readingagency.org.uk/quickreads

Continue your reading journey with The Reading Agency:

Reading Ahead

Challenge yourself to complete six reads by taking part in
Reading Ahead at your local library, college or workplace:
readingahead.org.uk

Book Club Hub

Join the **Book Club Hub** to find a book club and discover new
recommendations: **bookclubhub.co.uk**

World Book Night

Celebrate reading on **World Book Night,** every year on
23 April: **worldbooknight.org.uk**

Summer Reading Challenge

Read with your family as part of the **Summer Reading Challenge**:
summerreadingchallenge.org.uk

For more information on our work and the power
of reading visit: **readingagency.org.uk**

More from Quick Reads

If you enjoyed the 2026 Quick Reads, please explore our 6 titles from 2025:

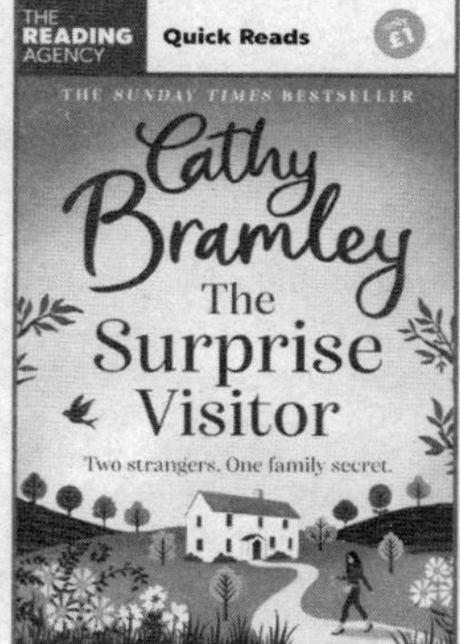

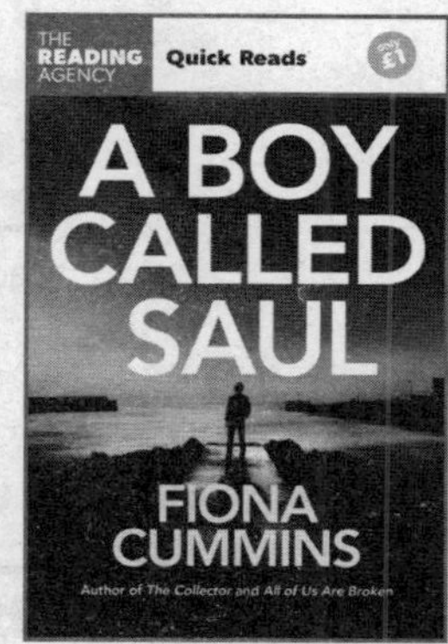

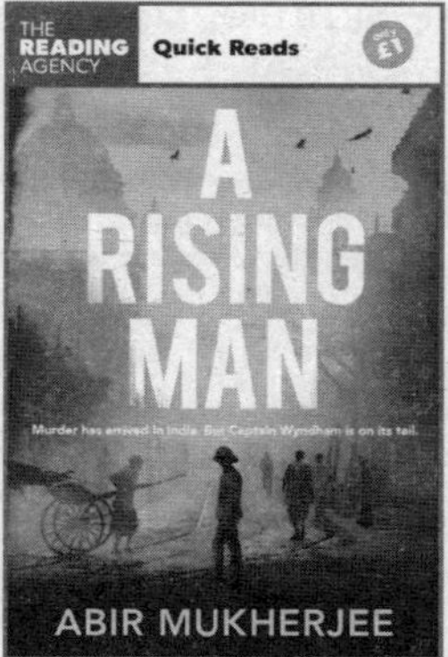

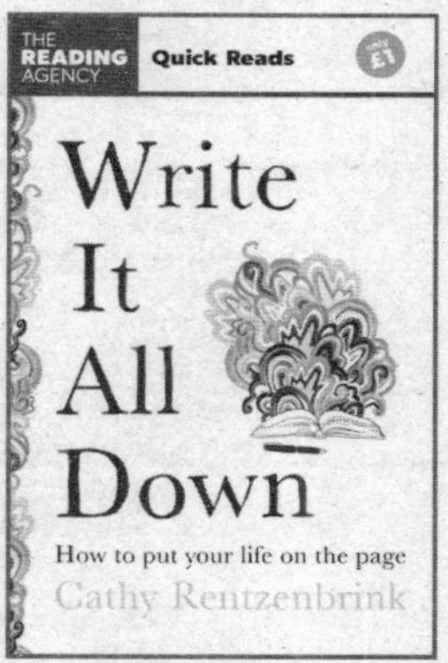

For a complete list of titles and more information on the authors and their books visit: **readingagency.org.uk/quickreads**

1 3 5 7 9 10 8 6 4 2

Vintage is part of the Penguin Random House group of companies

Vintage, Penguin Random House UK, One Embassy Gardens,
8 Viaduct Gardens, London SW11 7BW

penguin.co.uk/vintage
global.penguinrandomhouse.com

Penguin
Random House
UK

This Quick Reads edition published in in 2026

Set in 12/16 pt ITC Stone Serif Std
Typeset by Six Red Marbles UK, Thetford, Norfolk

Printed and bound in Great Britain by Clays Ltd, Elcograf S.p.A.

The authorised representative in the EEA is Penguin Random House Ireland,
Morrison Chambers, 32 Nassau Street, Dublin D02 YH68

A CIP catalogue record for this book is available from the British Library

ISBN 9781529990003

Penguin Random House is committed to a sustainable future
for our business, our readers and our planet. This book is made
from Forest Stewardship Council® certified paper.